Jimgrim and
the Seventeen thieves
of El-Kalil

Jimgrim and the Seventeen thieves of El-Kalil

by Talbot Mundy

Author of "The Iblis at Ludd," "The Lion of Petra," etc.
"The Woman Ayisha," copyright, 1922, by Talbot Mundy.

WILDSIDE PRESS

Published by
Wildside Press, LLC
www.wildsidepress.com

CHAPTER I

"Get the vote an' everything."

STEAM never killed Romance. It stalks abroad under the self-same stars that winked at Sinbad and Aladdin, and the only thing that makes men blind to it is the stupid craze for sitting in judgment on other people instead of having a good time with them.

"He who hates a thief is a thief at heart," runs the eastern proverb that nevertheless includes in its broad wisdom no brief at all for dishonesty.

If you hated thieves in El-Kalil you would be busy and, like the toad under the harrow, inclined to wonder where the gaps are; you can see the graves of the men who have tried it, in any direction, from any hill-top; and Romance, which knows nothing of any moral issue, comes at last with the liquid moonlight making even whited tombs look sociable. But it is better to be sociable while you live, if only for the sake of having some good yarns to tell the other fellows during pauses in between the rounds of feasting in Valhalla, when you get there. El-Kalil is Hebron of Old Testament fame — the oldest known city in the world apart and aloof in the Judean Hills — dirt delightful and without one trace of respect for anything but tradition, courage and cash.

Yet it was contrary to all tradition that an American citizen should be on his way there with almost unlimited authority to up-end everything, and, after spilling all the beans, to sort out the speckled undesirables. We ran into lots of courage, but it was fear of an uprising and its consequences that set the ball rolling. And as for hard cash, it was lack of it that brought the courage out, providing only two young men and some cigarettes wherewith to hold calm and lawful the most turbulently lawless city in the Near East.

Grim took me along for several reasons but the chief one was that he chose so to do.

Having been commissioned in the British army as an American, he had stuck to more than one national peculiarity, of which that first and the sweetest was doing as he gosh darn pleased as long as he could get away with it. Having made good all along that line, he could get away with almost any thing; and by that time, having risked a neck or two together, we were friends.

The second most important reason, I believe, was that he, and the few in authority over him, had discovered that I had no ax to grind. Life isn't worth while to me if I've got to worry over other people's morals or be a propagandist; to my way of looking at it, a man has a hard enough job to keep his own conscience from getting indigestion, while getting all the fun in sight, and there's no fun whatever in forcing your opinions on other folk. And the other fellow's job is difficult enough without our offering ignorant advice. Life's a great game and the measure of our own cussedness is the measure with which we get cussed. Amen.

So I had fitted unofficially into one or two tight places and officialdom was therefore pleased to let down the bars that restrain the general tourist. But there was a third reason: I was utterly unknown in Hebron, and it is the unknown entity that upsets most calculations, like the joker in a pack of cards.

There were likely enough other reasons, but I did not know them. Behold Grim and me on a blossomy May morning, mounted on two Bikaneeri camels left over from the war, swinging along the road to Hebron in gorgeous sunshine at a cushiony, contenting clip.

The camels were less conspicuous in that landscape than the regulation Ford car would have been and you can't travel fast enough even with gasoline to get ahead of the wind-borne word of mouth that ever since the Deluge has proved nearly as quick, if not quite so truthful always as the telegraph. To make us even less worth comment we wore the Arab costume that fits even a white man into the picture, and is comfortable past belief. Our other clothes were in the saddle-bags.

I know why the Jews want Palestine. I would want it too, if the world weren't so full of other things I haven't yet seen and admired. You feel like Abraham, on camel-back up in those hills, only without his responsibilities.

One of Abraham's direct descendants met us coming the other way, close to where the road winds by the Pools of Solomon. He was in a one-horse carriage of the mid-Victorian era, drawn by an alleged horse of about the same date or vintage. On his head was a Danbury-made Derby hat and he had a horse-shoe stick-pin in his necktie, his thumbs stuck into his suspenders and his feet on the seat in front. But he passed us the time of day in ancient Hebrew, and Grim, who has studied that language for Intelligence Department purposes, stopped to answer him.

At the end of half-a-dozen sentences it was obvious that Grim knew more of the language than the other did. The revival of dead speech takes time, and there are not so many in the country yet who can use the old tongue fluently although Zionists usually begin a conversation with it for propaganda purposes.

"Talk English," Grim suggested.

"What? You know English? Where d'you learn it?"

"In the States. Where else?"

"What? You lived in the States? What did you come back here for? Lots of room in the States for you fellers — good money — good living — get the vote an' everything. Where's your home now? Hebron?"

Grim nodded. The Jew pulled out a cigar.

"Well, I've just come from telling 'em in Hebron that they all ought to emigrate to the U.S.A."

"Would they listen?"

"Good listeners. They listened so good, they got my watch and chain while I was talkin', an' they'd have had my pocket-book if I hadn't locked it up in Jerusalem before I came away. Smoke cigars? Try this one. Say: if you come across a gold watch an' chain with the initials A.C. done on it in a monogram across the back, just send word to Aaron Cohen at the New Hotel Jerusalem, and there'll be a good reward for you. I went an' complained at the Governorate, but that schoolboy they've made governor can't do nothing about it. Take it from me, he's got no brains and no police-force. I'll buy the watch back and you tell 'em so — a good reward to whoever brings it, and no questions asked. Better have this cigar, hadn't you?"

But you don't smoke cigars on camel-back, at least not if you want to avoid being taken for a foreigner.

"Was the watch valuable?" Grim asked him.

"Would I worry about it if it was a cheap one? If it was a nine-carat case d'you think I'd have called the young governor all the names I did, and risk my life in the *suk* [Bazaar] afterwards against his orders, arguin' with a lot o' knifers? Eighteen-carat — twenty-two jewels — breguet spring — say: get me that watch back an' I'll give you twenty U.S. dollars for yourself!"

"Don't want 'em," said Grim, smiling down placidly from the superior height of the camel.

"What — you don't want dollars? Quit your kiddin'! There's nobody in this land don't want dollars."

"How badly d'you want that watch?"

"Oh, all right — twenty-five, then: but that's the limit."

"Dollars won't do. I know you for a good scout, Aaron Cohen, or I'd let you lose your watch for abusing young de Crespigny. That boy's got his hands full. How'd you like to be Governor of Hebron?"

"Not bloody likely! I'd sooner be King of the Irish! He's not a bad feller at that, only too thick with Arabs. He gave me a drink after I'd done criticizing. But say: what do you know about me?"

"And your emigration business? Nearly as much as you do!"

"Who are you, anyway?"

"My name is Grim."

"What? Him they call Jimgrim? Pardon me! Somehow I *thought* you didn't talk like an Arab. Well, you're the very man I'm looking for. I want my watch back, Major Grim. I've got no money in my pocket or I'd give it to you, but there's fifty dollars you can use however you please, and I'll pay it on your say-so — no questions asked. Could anything be fairer than that?"

"D'you want it badly enough to turn back?"

"What — to that nest o' thieves? To Hebron? To El-Kalil? Um-m-m! I got no money for one thing."

"I'll lend you whatever you need."

"Your risk! If they skin it from me, it's your money!"

"All right."

"You must have some mighty strong reason for wanting me back in Hebron!"

"I have. You'll be all right for a day or two. There's a hotel."

"Yey — I been there. The bugs in it have red-hot bear-traps on their feet and the food ain't fit for niggers!"

"Well, d'you want the watch?"

"You'll get it for me?"

"Yes, if you turn back."

"Uh! If you were English I wouldn't trust you; I'd say you were kiddin' yourself or kiddin' me. Go on, I'll take a chance."

"See you at the hotel then."

Grim and I rode on and in five minutes hardly the dust of Cohen's carriage was visible behind us.

We rode side by side, but it is not easy to talk from camel-back, although the beasts' feet make hardly any noise; I've a notion that the habitual reticence of the desert-folk is partly due to enforced silence for long periods on the march, when the swing and sway of the camels and the cloth over the rider's mouth make conversation next to impossible. Grim's information came in snatches.

"Good fellow, Cohen. Clever devil. Zionist. Thinks he can provide land here for Jews by encouraging Arabs to emigrate. Money behind him. Settle 'em on land in Arkansas and Tennessee. Kind fellow. Hot-air merchant. Good at bottom. Shrewd. Strange mixture of physical fear and impudent courage."

"What makes you so sure you can recover the watch?"

"Experience of Hebron. I was governor there once."

FOR an hour after that we padded along in silence through a country dotted with enormous herds of black goats in charge of patriarchal-looking shepherds. The only trees in sight were occasional ancient olives; but as we drew near Hebron the hillsides were all divided by stone walls into orchards and we passed between miles of grape-vines, interspersed with *mishmish,* as they call their apricots.

You don't see Hebron until the road begins to descend into it, and then the first view is of a neat modern village with the German influence predominant; for there, as everywhere else in Palestine, the Germans had not been content with making plans; they built good stone houses. The ancient city lies beyond all that, utterly untouched by science — a chaotic jumble flaunted in the face of discipline.

We stopped in front of the Governorate, and that, of course was a German building, a neat little residence with a garden in front and a stone wall all about it, in sight of the jail which, equally of course, was Turkish. The Turks built nothing so good as their jails and the Germans strengthened them, but it took the British to clean them of vermin, and filth and untried prisoners.

The Hebron jail is outside the city for more good reasons than one. Where ninety-nine per cent of a city's population is eligible for rigorous confinement on one ground or another and the cleverest thieves on earth are trained besides, no mere iron bars within the city limits would serve the purpose; you need open spaces all around for rifle and machine-gun fire — except of course, in famine time, when most of the population plans to be arrested and fed two square meals a day, at the foreign tax-payers' expense.

Captain de Crespigny came out of the Governorate to greet us, smiling all over as a man should whose only dependable assistant has the tooth-ache.

"You know the wire is down behind you?" he said pleasantly.

"Since when?"

"An hour ago. I'm rather worried about a Jew named Cohen. I let him start for Jerusalem this morning. 'Fraid now he may get scuppered on the way."

"It's all right; we met him. He's on his way back."

"Oh, did you get wind of trouble here?"

"Not a thing. Wanted Cohen here for a special reason. What's up?"

"I tried to phone through to Jerusalem for a machine gun. There's nobody to send. We've a motor-cycle, but it's *napoo*. That fellow Cohen lost his watch and I arrested a local Arab on suspicion soon after Cohen had gone. He's over there in the jail now and four thousand of his friends have sworn an oath to take him out again by force. I've ten policemen — one first-class man and nine with the wind up them."

"Are you sure the wire's down?" Grim asked him.

"Perfectly. I'd call that luck, only now you've come. They couldn't exactly have blamed me for bluffing the business through without orders and I think I could have tackled it. However, I suppose you take over?"

"Not if I know it!" Grim answered. "Make over to me when you've had enough, but no sooner."

"Thanks. Come in and have a drink. Who's your friend?"

"Ramsden — a countryman of mine."

Grim introduced me and for the hundredth time in that man's land I experienced the unmitigated delight of being accepted as an equal, instead of as a possibly objectionable person, on the strength of his mere say-so. As a general rule you can't get past that suave screen the British use to camouflage their real thoughts, without a guide whom they know and trust; but when you're in, you're in.

De Crespigny was nothing unusual; clean-shaven, almost always laughing about something, looking about twenty although really twenty-six, probably not brilliant, but capable of swift judgment and astounding impudence in tight places. Obviously one of those well-bred young gentlemen, who have kept an empire's borders by daring and straight dealing while the politicians did the bragging and the profiteers made hay. He wore several ribbons for distinguished service, but the only thing he seemed really proud of was a mixture he called a Hebron cocktail, made without ice from a recipe of his own invention.

It was a comfortable room we entered, for the Germans had left their furniture behind them and the walls were hung besides with deadly weapons taken away from the local cut-throats by this de Crespigny child, his one assistant, the one bold native policeman and the "nine with the wind up them."

THE assistant came in while we watched the secret ritual of cocktail shaking in an ex-beer bottle; another boy, two years younger than his chief and, barring the tooth-ache, even more amused by the certainty that mass-murder was afoot. You could sum him up instantly. When a man thinks of his job first, and tooth-ache merely as a handicap, bet on him. Besides his name was Jones and that is a well-known label.

"Just come from the jail," he announced. "Had to put Ali ben Hamza in a cell by himself; he was propaganding among the other prisoners. Perfectly friendly, though; assured me that you and I will both be dead before morning and offered to pull my tooth out with his fingers. Said he hated to see me suffer and that having your throat cut doesn't hurt a bit."

"Thought you were going to the doctor," said de Crespigny.

"No time. He has his hands full anyhow. Hospital's chock-a-block, and no one to help him operate. Any news?"

"Wire's down."

"Oh, good! That means Jerusalem can't interfere and tell us not to do things. But —" glancing at Grim and me "— are you still in charge, 'Crep?"

"I've no orders to take over," Grim assured him. "De Crespigny may pass the buck when he sees fit."

"Pretty decent of you."

"Suppose you fellows put me wise, though," Grim suggested. "We'll call it unofficial, but in case of need it might be wholesome for me to know the facts."

"It's all very simple," said de Crespigny. "Aaron Cohen came here with a scheme for exporting Arabs to your country to make room for Jews. He offers to buy out their holdings for cash, to arrange their passage to the States, get passports for them and all that, and provide them with good land to settle on at the other end on easy terms. Perfectly fair and above-board if they wanted to do it, but they don't.

"On top of that, the Jews in this place are Orthodox and hate the Zionists worse than they do pork. They made the mistake of telling the Arabs that Cohen was no good, whereas he's quite a decent fellow really, if it weren't for his infernal cheek. No need to tell *you* what the Moslems of this place are like. They stole Cohen's watch for a joke and he said what he thought of them. They admit the truth of all he said — you know how engagingly frank they are about themselves — but take exception to criticism by any kind of Jew.

"Now they say that the Orthodox Jews put Cohen up to it and only went back on him afterwards because they were afraid. They say it's really the Orthodox Jews of this place who are planning to get their holdings; and as most of them owe money to the Jews they propose to make short work of the lot of them. They've cut the wire to prevent our phoning for Sikhs and machine guns and the game is probably scheduled to begin tonight."

Before de Crespigny had finished speaking two men came into the room and one of them, obviously a middle-aged Scotsman, sat down without waiting to be invited. The other, an Arab long past middle age, remained standing. Grim made a sign to me that I interpreted as a call to behave in keeping with the Arab costumes we were wearing and I hid my face as much as I reasonably could in the folds of the *kufiyi*.

"*Allah ysabbak bilkhair!* [God give you a happy morning!]" the old Arab began as soon as he could get a word in.

"*Ahlan wasah'lan!* [A thousand times welcome!]" said de Crespigny. "What is it, Yussuf?"

"You young men go! Go to your mothers! Go home and marry wives!"

"Why this sudden interest in our future, Yussuf?"

"It is not sudden. I am an old man, and have seen many young men die. I have yet to see the good that came of killing them. Go home."

"Men die when their time comes," said de Crespigny. "Moreover, they don't marry wives in my land until the woman is willing. I've got no money and the girls won't look at me."

"It is not good to answer with jests when an old man speaks in earnest. I, who must see death soon in the natural course of things, advise you as a father speaking to his sons. Go home. It is better to beget sons than to die young."

"You old raven! What are you croaking about?"

The Arab stroked his gray beard and thought a minute before he answered. Then:

"I have seen the blood flow in the runnels of the streets of El-Kalil like red storm-water. I was here when the Turks took vengeance on the city for certain matters. I have seen the seven districts of the city at war with one another and the executions afterwards. All those are as nothing in comparison to what comes! It is written that not one Jew shall remain alive in El-Kalil!"

"Any date to that prophecy?" asked de Crespigny quite calmly.

"They are whetting the swords now!"

"They'll have us to reckon with before they begin on the Jews."

"Truly, my son. Therefore go, before the sacrifice begins! What can you few do against so many? Can you send for help? I think not. I am told the wire is cut. Could a horseman or man on foot get through to Jerusalem alive? Not he! They would let you escape, but not your messenger; and if you stay, you die!"

"Supposing I chose to run away, they'd be fools to let me," de Crespigny answered. "There'd be lorry-loads of Sikhs here two or three hours after I reached Jerusalem."

"And the Sikhs will bury the dead Jews! Listen, my son. You British are not Turks. Who in this place is afraid of British vengeance, after living under the Turk's heel so many years? The Sikhs will come and shoot a handful. There will be a trial, at which every witness will tell lies. Those who have the fewest friends will be convicted; some will be hanged and some imprisoned. For four thousand Jews slain will forty Moslems hang? Better go before the sacrifice begins!"

"You go back into the city," said de Crespigny, as calmly as if he were ordering the streets cleaned, "and tell your friends this: There's only one authority in this place, and that's me! Say they have me to deal with before they can start on the Jews!"

"You and these few and ten policemen!" The old Arab smiled and spread out his hands in a gesture of something like despair. "They will go first to the jail, pillage it and set the prisoners free. Next they will come here, for there are rifles here and cartridges. In less time than the muezzin needs to cry his summons they will slay you and take the rifles. After, the Jews! And after that, if it is written that the Sikhs shall come, then that is written, and who shall stay the hand of God?"

"Go and tell them to come here first before they try the jail," said de Crespigny calmly. "That is all I have to say. Go and tell them."

"*Allah ysallmak!* [God save you!]" said the Arab sadly.

"*Allah yihfazak!* [God keep you!]" de Crespigny replied, and the old man turned and went.

"Doc," said de Crespigny, turning toward the Scotsman, "there are two camels outside. Better take them. Put Miss Gordon on one and you and she make a break for Jerusalem. This situation looks none too good."

Doctor Cameron laughed dryly, wrinkling up his eyes as he looked keenly at each of us in turn. He was a big man, with a powerful head and a firm, good-tempered mouth under a scraggly gray moustache. He looked like an old soldier, but had never actually worn any other uniform than the mask and apron of the operating-room.

"Five-and-twenty years I've been here," he replied. "Can you see me running away?"

"But the nurse — Miss Gordon?"

"She's a fine girl. She'll stand by. Ask her if you'd rather. I'll not interfere."

"Better send her to this place, then."

"You young Hector! She's safer in my hospital. They'll do no murder there; we're far too useful to them. I stood by them through the war as a Turks' prisoner; they'll remember that. There's hardly a man in Hebron hasn't been to me for help at one time or another. But what do you lads propose to do?"

"Brazen it out," said de Crespigny.

"You'll need all your brass, I'm thinking." He looked hard at Jones. "That boy's in no fit state to give the best that's in him. I brought my bag with me. Let me see that lower jaw."

He took Jones' head in capable, enormous hands and tilted it toward the light.

"Open. Wider. Um-m-m! Sit on that stool. Reach me the bag, de Crespigny."

He unwrapped a lancet and a pair of ugly forceps, then got behind Jones and gripped his head firmly between his knees.

"By rights ye ought to have an anaesthetic for a job like this, but your mother had to endure a lot worse when ye came into the world. We'll see if you're half as good a man as your mother. Now!"

It was a bloody business and not convenient to watch, but we all looked on like spectators at a play, pretending not to feel the skin creep up our spines. It was several minutes before the last piece of a broken tooth was tossed into the brass basin that a servant brought.

"Now lie down. If I ever meet your mother I'll tell the lady that her labor was worth while. Ye'll feel finely by and by. He might have an ounce or two of whisky."

He wrapped up his tools, turned down his shirt-sleeves, and started for the door.

"If I can be of any further use, my boys, ye'll know where to find me. The best advice I can give is, always let the Arab know you're not afraid of him, and make him suspect ye've something in reserve. And by the way — ye'd better all join me at the hospital, if things look too bad. I think the rascals will respect that place. There'll be bad news from Jerusalem before night or my name isn't Cameron."

De Crespigny glanced swiftly at Grim. Grim nodded. That was puzzling, for there had been no signs of disturbance that I could see when we came away that morning.

Cameron jerked his head and snapped his fingers in the doorway. "They'd never talk so bold here if they didn't know of trouble brewing in Jerusalem to keep the troops occupied," he said, and strode out as if any sort of trouble were the merest commonplace.

I found it utterly impossible, sitting in that quiet room, to believe that we were in imminent danger; but that may have been because I had no official job to lose if everything should go wrong. A man doesn't fear for his life as a rule until the raw facts stare him in the face; it is economic and administrative problems that cause terror in advance. I thought that even Grim, who hardly ever shows more emotion than the proverbial red Indian in times of stress, looked serious.

And some one else arrived just then, who took no trouble to conceal his feelings. Aaron Cohen had himself announced by the Arab servant and followed him into the room without waiting for an invitation. He did not speak at first, but stood looking from one to the other of us with an expression on his face mixed of comedy and desperation.

"Nice way to bring a feller back to this place!" he said at last. "I went to the hotel and they wouldn't let me in. Said they'd trouble enough in store without me. Gave me a fine talk, they did. Pogrom — that's the name of it! Down at that hotel they're saying all the Jews in Hebron will be dead before morning and they're blaming me for it. What have I done?" He faced Grim and glared at him. "D'you call that acting on the level, to bring me back to this place when you knew what was in the air?"

"You'd never have reached Jerusalem alive," said de Crespigny.

"Has that young feller been knifed?" asked Cohen, pointing at Jones on the couch. He was still spitting blood at intervals, so the question was excusable.

"Sit down, Cohen," Grim answered. "You're as safe here as anywhere at present. Will you have his bag brought in, de Crespigny? Now, Cohen, you didn't start this trouble, but your talk brought it to a head. It's up to us to smooth the thing out if we can, but it's going to be no joking matter. I'm asking you to keep quiet and to help us if there's an opportunity. Will you?"

"Sure, I'll help," said Cohen. "But what can I do?"

"Dunno yet," Grim answered. "Captain de Crespigny's in charge. We'll see."

CHAPTER II

"These are two good boys."

THE Scots doctor's prognostications were proven accurate sooner than expected. Rumor travels on swallow's wings in that land and almost as soon as Cohen's bag had been carried in there came a native policeman looking pallid under the bronze, who saluted precisely and then talked to de Crespigny and Jones with the familiarity of an old nurse to children.

"Word has come that the Jews in Jerusalem are massacring Moslems! Shall ten of us prevent the Moslems here from turning the tables on the Jews? Better let it be known at once that we intend to stand aside. Then let them get the business over with. Afterward will be the proper time to make arrests."

He looked like a perfectly good policeman, but there had not been time enough yet to educate out of him Turkish notions of convenience.

"Who brought the news?" asked de Crespigny.

"He is outside."

"Bring him in."

A burly-looking ruffian with more white to his eye than sheer straightforwardness begets, clad in a smelly sheepskin coat and with a long knife tucked into his sash, was ushered in and stood uncomfortably in the middle of the room.

"Are you from Jerusalem?" de Crespigny asked him.

"Yes."

"Since when?"

"I have just come."

"And you left Hebron after seven o'clock this morning to my knowledge! Have you got so virtuous and truthful that you've suddenly grown wings?"

"I went half-way and met three men, who said the Jews of Jerusalem have risen and have already killed three thousand Moslems. So I came back."

"To talk about it, eh? Well, if I hear of your repeating such a lie in Hebron I'll clap you in the jail, d' you understand me? Go home and hold your tongue."

"Taib [All right]."

The man slouched out again, but three more reports arrived by way of the back door within the next ten minutes, the last one giving the total of slain at exactly four thousand eight hundred and one Moslems, adding that the Jews were parading through Jerusalem in triumph.

"All of which probably means that a Jew has been killed and the Moslems are looting," Grim commented quietly.

The next alarm was a message from the Arab jailer to say that his prisoners were getting out of hand and that a crowd was collecting outside the jail.

Jones volunteered to go and investigate, but before he could leave the room two policemen came running in with word that the crowd was swarming up-street toward the Governorate. We could hear them a moment later. They were taking their time about it, singing as they came, pausing at intervals to dance a few steps in measure and then surging on. The song was like the Carmagnole of the Terror. De Crespigny got up from his chair — thought better of it — sat down again and lighted a cigarette. After that he passed the case around and we each took one, Cohen included.

"What's going to happen?" asked Cohen. "Those guys coming to kill us?" He looked less afraid than I felt. "Well, I guess it's up to you fellers to fix this."

"I'll go out and talk to them," said de Crespigny.

"Take your time," Grim advised him. "Let them wait for you."

It was obvious that de Crespigny and Jones felt better for Grim's being there, although to my mind he was stretching his policy of non-interference to absurd limits. I had seen enough of his influence with Arabs at one time and another to convince me that he could do nearly what he liked with them and I itched to tell him to take charge and use his resourceful wits. He made no move whatever, but sat like a wooden Indian in front of a tobacco store, blowing out the cigarette-smoke through his nose.

The crowd — there must have been two or three thousand of them — came thundering up-street, chanting over and over again a rape-and-murder chorus in response to the stanzas of a solo sung by a man who was carried shoulder-high in their midst waving a sword. I could see his sword through the window, over the top of the shrubs and the stone wall. They halted in front of the gate and the song ceased. In the silence that followed when the shuffling of feet had died down you could hear them breathe.

"I suppose they'll swipe our camels?" I suggested.

"Not yet," Grim answered. "They'll do nothing much yet unless they think we're rattled. Take your time, de Crespigny."

The Governor of Hebron got out of his chair again with all the stately dignity of twenty-six amusing years, and lighted another cigarette with a deliberately steady hand.

"Do I look as if I'd got the wind up me, or any rot like that?" he asked.

"You look good," Grim assured him. "Be sure you smile, though. You'll pull it off all right."

"Shall I come with you?" asked Jones.

"No. Better not. They might think we were scared, if two of us went. So long."

De Crespigny walked out, doing the most difficult thing in the world perfectly, which is to act exactly like your normal self when fear is prompting you to bluster and look preternaturally clever. Jones began talking in a matter-of-fact voice to Cohen about his emigration scheme.

"Care to come with me?" asked Grim; and he and I went upstairs to watch from a bedroom window, screening ourselves carefully behind the curtains.

"These are two good boys," said Grim. "More depends on them than you guess. If they can hold Hebron quiet for two days, all's well. If not, the next thing will be a march on Jerusalem, and every Moslem in the country is likely to follow suit."

"Couldn't the British machine guns deal with that?"

"Of course. But who wants to slaughter 'em?"

"Pity the wire's down," said I.

"Uh-uh! Wouldn't be any good. All the troops Jerusalem could spare would only whet these fellows' appetites for blood. Judging by the symptoms before we came away I should say Jerusalem will have its hands full for the next forty-eight hours or so. But watch de Crespigny."

THE crowd in the street was packed so densely that those nearest were pressed against the gate and de Crespigny could not open it. There was only one gap in their midst, where one of our camels lay and the other stood moving his jaw phlegmatically. Camels get excited only when they shouldn't, and insist on taking human climaxes with the indifference they possibly deserve; those two beasts were the only meditative creatures within view, although the crowd was silent enough — sweating in the hot sun — a sea of faces set in the white frames of *kufiyis,* angry, but intensely anxious to know what this youngster of an alien race proposed to do.

De Crespigny did not hesitate. He vaulted on to the wall, stood on it for a minute to judge the number of the crowd and get a bird's-eye view of what was happening on its outskirts, then sat down on the wall facing them, with his feet hanging on a level with their breasts. They could have seized him easily. A fool would have stood up and tried to look dignified out of reach.

"Now, don't all speak at once," he began. "What do you want?"

Of course they all did speak at once, at the top of their lungs for the most part and he waited until the tumult died.

"Suppose one or two of you speak for the rest," he suggested at last.

A burly man of middle age took that duty on himself and de Crespigny had to draw his legs up, for the men in front were crushed tight against the wall by those behind who wanted to hear better. So he set his feet on the shoulders of the men beneath him and they seemed rather to like it.

"We are told that the Jews in Jerusalem are murdering our co-religionists!"

"I've heard that story too," said de Crespigny. "If it's true, it's bad."

"Give us rifles, then! We are going to Jerusalem to help our friends!"

"I wouldn't do that if I were you. The military might mistake your motive; then there'd be an accident. Let's find out the truth first; I'm as keen to know it as you are. Tell you what: the wire's down, so I can't phone, but see those two camels. Why don't you choose two men whose word you can depend on, let them take those camels, and bring back word? I'll write a pass that will get them by the guard outside Jerusalem; and I'll give them a letter asking the authorities to let them see what's happening. How about it?"

The sweet reasonableness of that offer was too much even for their fanaticism, but there were men at the back of the crowd to whom it did not appeal for various reasons — the chief of them, no doubt, that it postponed the hour of looting.

"Ali Baba ben Hamza is in the jail on a Jew's complaint!" they yelled. "Let him out! Give him back to us!"

"Certainly not!" laughed de Crespigny. "I've had most of you in the jail at one time or another! Which of you was ever jailed unfairly? Ali Baba ben Hamza stays in until he's had a fair trial. Anything else?"

"How do we know the Jews in the jail haven't killed him already?"

"You know quite well I'd never let them. There are only three Jews in the jail, and Ali Baba has a cell to himself. However — choose a committee of five or six of you, and I'll issue a permit for the committee to visit him and make sure."

"Let him out! Let him out!"

"Certainly not! Choose your committee if you want to. But you're wasting time. Send two men to Jerusalem on the camels and bring us all back that news."

"Kill him!" yelled some one from behind, but no other voice repeated it and the man who had made the suggestion was elbowed further to the rear. De Crespigny pretended not to have heard.

"I could recognize that fellow again," said I.

"Never mind him," Grim answered.

"You'd all better go away now and wait in your homes until the camels get back," said de Crespigny. "I'll see the head-men inside the city in the *mejliss* [council] hall half an hour from now. Take care that all the head-men come! Who are going on the camels? What are their names?"

It did not take them a minute to choose delegates, for among Arabs there never seems any doubt as to which man's evidence is to be preferred before that of others. De Crespigny took their names, vaulted off the wall, and went into the house to write a pass for them. Before he returned with it the crowd had already begun to disperse, relieving the pressure so that he could open the gate this time and go out among them. The pass was written in English for the benefit of British sentries, but he read it aloud to the nearest men, translating into Arabic to satisfy them that they were not being tricked; and the moment the camel-men were off the crowd went too, in the opposite direction. They seemed to have forgotten about Ali Baba ben Hamza in the jail.

"That gives us eight hours' breathing space at all events," de Crespigny laughed when we rejoined him in the room downstairs. "Next question is what to do with it. I'll interview the head-men presently and use strong language, but what after that?"

"Stage a side-show," Grim answered.

"Easy to say, but what? How?"

"Suppose we call that my end?" Grim suggested.

"All right, sir. That'll suit me." De Crespigny turned to Jones. "How's the jaw now? I think perhaps you'd better show yourself in the city. Walk about the place and show them we're not panicky; it'll do our policemen as much good as any one to see we're cool and on the job. How many men are on guard outside the jail?"

"Three."

"Take one away. Tell the other two they're such fine fellows that two's plenty. Let the third man walk through the streets behind you, it'll do his guts good. I'll stroll about too, after I've seen the head-men. Meet here for dinner, eh? Leave you to your own devices, I suppose?" he added, smiling cheerfully at Grim.

"Yes. I shall visit the jail first. So long."

Cohen heaved a huge sigh as de Crespigny and Jones walked out.

"Eight hours, eh? Well, that's something! But why, if two o' them knifers can go to Jerusalem on camels, can't some other feller go and ask for troops? What this place needs is Sikhs — lots of 'em, with the corks off the end o' their bayonets! Why not indent for a regiment quick an' lively?"

"Because," Grim answered slowly, "they've plenty to worry them just now in Jerusalem without our adding to it. The troops at Ludd are being held in readiness to go elsewhere and all the men in Jerusalem are hardly enough to keep order. If we can't handle this without the Sikhs, we're 'it,' that's all."

"And you're going out? And him? He going with you? I'm to sit alone in this place? What d'you take me for?"

"A man."

"Say; I'll go with you to the jail!"

"Uh-uh! Jews indoors just now! If the Arabs were to fall foul of you and draw blood, there'd be no stopping them. Sit here and read. You'll be all right."

I felt strong sympathy for Cohen. Perhaps what Grim had said of him while we were on the way had something to do with that, but I think I would have liked him in any case, not being one of those unfortunates so prejudiced that they loathe Jews simply because there was once a man named Judas. There were and are others.

Grim was obviously working him thoughtfully, no doubt in order to bring to the top the particular quality or mood he then had use for — that being Grim's way. I have never known him try to convert a man, or waste much time on futile argument; so far as I have been able to analyze Grim's method from close study of it, I should say he accepts the world exactly as he finds it and then looks keenly for something he can use. He invariably seems to find it somewhere in the heap, although not by any means always on top.

"Doin' things is easy," Cohen grumbled. "Sittin' still expectin' things to happen is what eats you."

"All the same, sit here," Grim answered. "There'll be plenty for you to do presently. We shall need the use of your wits and all your pluck. Out in the street they'd very likely kill you and I've never seen a dead man's brains real active. I'm off to get your watch."

"Shucks! Let 'em keep it! Don't get startin' more trouble!"

"Did you ever see a forest fire in the States checked by setting another one?"

Grim answered. "Sit tight, Cohen; we'll be back for dinner."

But we did not start out in the Arab clothes we were still wearing. Upstairs in de Crespigny's bedroom Grim got into his major's uniform and I changed into flannels — it was hot enough for a bathing suit. The room was full of curios de Crespigny had picked up in the course of eight years' foreign service and Grim used up a minute or two studying a picture of Japanese Shintoist priests performing the "Hi-Watterai" stunt of walking barefooted on a bed of burning charcoal.

"Who was it said that about the world being full of a number of things?" he remarked. "Are you ready? Come on."

In the street he began to let fall little scraps of information in that aggravating way he has, that starts you conjecturing and guessing until you realize that you know less than you thought you did before.

"This old Ali Baba ben Hamza that de Crespigny has put in jail is the very man I left Jerusalem to come and see. He's the father of Mahommed ben Hamza, who helped us at El-Kerak you remember, and again to some extent at Ludd. The old boy has sixteen sons and grandsons, and they're about the toughest gang this side of Chicago. If they've got Cohen's watch we ought to be able to stave off a holy war."

"I never heard anything sound more like a complete *non sequitur,*" said I.

"Thieving has been a poor trade in Hebron lately," he answered. "When professional thieves come on hard times, Ramsden, they pray for trouble as a rule and usually help to start it, with a view to loot. There've been strange doings by night in this town of late. Let's hope Doc Cameron has plenty of chemicals."

"What on earth for?"

"We've got to stage a bluff or go fluey."

It was not far to the jail and there were not many people in the street to see us pass; but those who did see us recognized Grim and were respectful, if not exactly obviously glad to know he was in town. I saw one man go running off in the direction of the city to carry the news.

The jail was a long stone structure with a stone roof and iron-barred windows, looking not altogether unlike an American armory on a small scale. The two dark-gray-uniformed policemen on guard outside it became suddenly possessed by a new spirit at sight of Grim and beamed at him as they presented arms. He stopped for a minute to address each of them by name and make some familiar joke in Arabic.

"Nothing to be afraid of," he assured them.

They laughed, shrugged their shoulders and seemed to revert at once to their former state of gloom.

"If only there were Sikhs here! Our two officers are very young and there are only ten of us! The men in the city are calling us traitors, being Moslems born in this place yet taking the pay and obeying the orders of the British, who are foreigners! And now come these tales from Jerusalem! We are willing to die like men but, in the name of God, Jimgrim, this is no joking matter!"

"Who am I, that you should think I joke about it?" Grim answered. "I am a foreigner. I take the pay and obey the orders of the British. They and you and I are here to keep the peace, that is all. Our honor is concerned in the matter. There is more honor in being ten than ten thousand, when the ten are right and the others wrong. As for the youth of your officers — which would you prefer, young capables or old fools?"

"True — true, Jimgrim! We will stand! Depend on us!"

"Those fellows' property would be the first to be looted, if looting should begin," said Grim as we entered the jail. "It's a Hell of a test for men who were fighting for the Turks two years ago! The rest of us think we're men of principle and all that, but we don't know what temptation is! I'd like to know I was as brave as one of those policemen."

The jail was as clean as the proverbial new pin, divided up on the Turkish system into stone-floored cells, with room in each for twenty or thirty miserables on occasion, although now there were only two or three men clad in coarse jail suits who peered through each barred door curiously. They looked fat and on the whole not dissatisfied.

THE cell we sought was at the far end, and it seemed empty; but the Arab jailer who had followed us unlocked it and slammed the iron door shut again in a hurry behind us, as if afraid some wild beast might escape. Yet all we found inside was a meek-looking old patriarch with a long blue-gray beard, who sat in a corner telling amber beads so piously that he could hardly spare us attention. They had not dressed him in a jail suit; he was arrayed in all the full-flowing Arab dignity that is very far from being a mere mask. It is the outward and visible sign of an inner quality that makes those who know the Arab well prefer to condone his roguery.

"*Mar'haba,* Ali Baba!"

"*Allah y'afik,* Jimgrim! It is time! Behold the indignity to which that young whelp of an Englishman has put me! I have grandsons older than him! Yet he put me in this cell, laughing when I cursed him, as if an old man's curse had no weight. When I threatened him, he offered me tobacco — the young spawn of an adder! Tell the jailer to bring in two chairs, Jimgrim, and some tea, so that I can offer you hospitality! You and your friends will all be dead by midnight, but what of it? There is no malice between me and thee. Speak through the door to the jailer."

CHAPTER III

GRIM sat down on one of the clean stone floor-slabs and leaned his back against the wall.

"It is not good, Ali Baba, to see you in this place," he said.

"*Mashallah!* It is easy to spare your feelings, Jimgrim. Say the word to the jailer and you shall see me in the street in a minute!"

I sat down opposite and watched. Grim's expression was wholly of good humor, but under the old Arab's mask of friendly dignity I thought I could detect suppressed excitement. His eyes — soft-brown as a doe's — had fire behind them and he kept on telling his beads automatically, flicking each one forward with his thumb, as if in some way that relieved internal pressure.

"Have you been searched?" Grim asked him unexpectedly.

"No. I have suffered all indignities but that. *Inshallah* [If God wills], I shall be spared the searching and the prison bath."

"Suppose you give me Aaron Cohen's watch, then."

Grim held his hand out. The Arab shook his head.

"The Jew's watch? To the Devil with the Jew and the watch as well! I know nothing of either of them."

"I suppose," said Grim considerately, "when a man gets to your age, Ali Baba, his memory usually fails. Well, never mind; here is a nice clean cell, where you can sit and refresh your memory. Meditation may bring recollection. There is no hurry."

"Truly no hurry! Before dawn I shall be free. If the Jew still needs a watch by that time, the thing can be buried with him."

"You think the crowd is coming to release you, eh?"

The old man nodded.

"You are wrong," said Grim.

"If not tonight, then tomorrow night."

"That would bring sure eventual disaster on themselves, if they try to take you out of here by force."

"Am I not Ali Baba? They will come."

"Ali Baba, the thief!"

"Ali Baba ben Hamza, the captain of thieves!"

The old man made that boast as proudly as ever Roman captain gloried in his legion, and Grim smiled comprehendingly.

"You're not going to be here when they come, old friend. We'll save them the trouble of pulling the jail down."

"Ah! That is wisest, Jimgrim. To spoil this good jail were a pity.

And there are mean rascals in here whom they would release, but who ought to remain for the hangman. It is best to let me go; you were always a man of discernment."

"Who mentioned letting you go?" Grim retorted, letting his face grow suggestively harder. "There is a less troublesome way than that."

"Allah! *Shi muhal?* [What does this talk mean?] You would hang me? You?"

"Not necessarily — at least, not yet. Do you think you know me?"

"As a father his son; as a farmer knows the weather; as a fox the hunter! Were you not once governor here?"

"Am I a liar?"

"Nay. A deceiver. A cunning and most bold contriver and twister of surprises. A man who smothers knowledge under smiles. A follower of dark ways. A danger, because of great subtlety and daring. But no liar. When you say a thing, Jimgrim, whoever has good sense believes it."

"Believe me now, then. You shall hang before you are rescued. Neither your sixteen sons and grandsons, nor any mob incited by them, shall get you alive out of our hands."

"Allah! You talk boldly, Jimgrim!"

"I have pledged my word."

"*Shu halalk!* [What talk is this!] I know the situation. Jerusalem can spare no troops. There is going to be short shrift in El-Kalil, and none can prevent it. Nevertheless, you shall have the Jew's watch, if that is all you want of me."

"It is not all."

"Then what else?"

"Give me the watch first."

"It is not here. On my honor, Jimgrim, in the name of the Most High God and of his Prophet, it is not here!"

"I thought not. Let me feel under your girdle. Not there? Under your arm? No. In the leg of your pantaloons then? Ah! I knew I'd heard it ticking."

Grim drew up the old man's cotton trousers and exposed the hairy leg. The watch was suspended by its gold chain just below the knee.

"So that's attended to. Now we'll go out of here and make you more comfortable at the Governorate. Cohen is there. You may give him the watch yourself if you'd rather."

"You will take me to the Governorate? *Taib!* [All right!] They will burn that place down instead of this!"

"All right, they'd better. Cost less. Come along."

Grim called the jailer, who let us out in a hurry and seemed more glad to be rid of that mild-looking old gentleman than if he had horns and a tail; but he took care to have Grim make the necessary entries in the prison book, and returned to Ali Baba the sweetest, silvery, long, gold-handled dagger in an ivory sheath that ever I set eyes on. I offered to buy it from him right away, but he saw only humor in that.

"You shall have it in your belly before morning!" he assured me. "Keep your money until then!"

Take him on the whole, he was the most delightful rascal I had met in Palestine. It was a sheer pleasure to walk the street in his company, Grim on one side and I on the other, lest he take it into that old splendid head of his to make a break for liberty. The very stride of the man was poetry; every gesture was romance. He was inconvertible to modern ways and incorruptible by modern thought — past history incarnate and unwilling to depart from ancient manners; as conventional in his own way as any of the ancient kings who once made war on Abraham.

Y OU would have thought he owned the Governorate by the way he entered it and the lecture he gave Aaron Cohen before returning his watch might have been taken out of the Book of Genesis.

"A rash man and his goods are like the wheat and the chaff," he told him. "A wind blows and they are separated. Yet there is compassion even for fools, and the heart of the wise discerns it. I am not willing to be enriched with your goods, lest you should meditate envy and bring evil into the world; for the little are envious and only the great have understanding. I give you back your watch."

"Is he to have the fifty dollars for it?" Cohen asked. "A feller with a nerve like him don't need money, but I'll stand by what I said to you."

"Does he speak of money? Tell him to think rather on damnation that awaits him after death!" said Ali Baba, turning his back. "I offered you tea in the jail, Jimgrim."

Grim chuckled.

"Shall I order tea? It's too bad the Koran forbids wine."

"Whisky is not wine. I have read the Koran through two hundred times and never found the word whisky mentioned in it."

Grim set a whisky bottle down on the table in front of him and the old man helped himself to a tumblerful.

"Now," said Grim, "we'll send for your sixteen sons and grandsons. Write them an invitation." He set paper and ink in front of him and looked on, smiling like the Sphinx.

"No, that won't do. Try again. Take another sheet. Nothing about politics this time. Tell them you're out of jail and quite comfortable in the Governorate as my guest. Say you've some advice to give them and that they can come without fear, all sixteen of them."

"But they will be busy. They are preparing certain matters."

"I know it. I won't interfere. They may go away afterward and make all the preparations they like."

Ali Baba wrote painstakingly and passed the finished note to Grim, who studied it for half a minute before calling a servant.

"To Mahommed ben Hamza in the *suk*. Come straight back here. Don't wait for an answer or stop to answer questions."

The man went off at a run and Grim sat down in the window-seat.

"Come and sit by me, Ali Baba. Now, you infernal old scoundrel, let's understand each other. I'm going to watch you like a fox stalking a bird, and I warn you not to make one signal to your gang. If you want to know what I'll do if you disobey me, just make one signal to your gang and see! These boys here made a mistake, didn't they, when they clapped you in jail? That gave you a chance to stir ructions, didn't it? And get rescued and fill your caves with loot after the rioting. Well, you'll tell that gang of yours that you're out of jail now, so that part of the program that called for an attack on the jail is off — absolutely off — you understand?"

Ali Baba nodded. His eyes were watching Grim's intently, trying to read the plan behind the spoken word.

"They'll ask you whether you're free yet. You'll answer what?"

"I am not free — *yet!*"

"No. That's the wrong answer. By the time they get here you will be free."

"*Taib!* I am willing! I will go with them."

"Yes. But you and I will have a private understanding first."

What struck me most as I watched the faces of the two men was a difference less of nationality and thirty years or so than of a couple of dozen centuries. And in spite of cunning and cocksureness won by half a century of practically unpunished and profitable crime; in spite of the fact, clear enough by now, that the Arab could count confidently on thousands of his fanatical friends to use direct force against us, who were an insignificant handful, for the moment out of reach of help, the impersonation of past history looked helpless against the young American.

I suspected Grim of being up to his old game of spotting the spark of elemental decency that is always hidden somewhere and fanning it into flame for his own use. Cohen, who knew Arabic better than I did, seemed equally aware of re-enforcements not yet seen. The expression on the Jew's face was of masked alertness, as distinguished from Grim's businesslike good humor.

"I know your game," said Grim. "See if I don't. There's a Moslem insurrection in Jerusalem, of which you've had full advance particulars. There's trouble in Egypt and Constantinople that keeps the army at Ludd under orders for instant service elsewhere; some one has told you of that, too. I'll deal with that some one later. You've had it in for the Jews here for a long time —"

"*Fi idak!* [That is certainly true!] They lend money to Moslems and collect the debts in the governor's court! It is forbidden by the Koran to lend money at usury."

"And you figure that the moment is therefore auspicious for a massacre."

"*Haida haik* [Quite true]. It is going to take place."

"You know there will be punishment afterward."

"Perhaps that is written."

"But as you don't propose to murder any Jews yourself, or at any rate don't intend to be seen murdering them, and have plenty of friendly witnesses in any case, you yourself expect to get off scot-free with lots of loot. Isn't that so?"

"I shall prove an alibi."

"I know you will! I'm going to help you!"

"*Mashallah!* What does this talk mean?"

"You have a son, by name Mahommed ben Hamza."

"Truly. My youngest. He will be here soon."

"When I came here to act as governor a year ago, he was in the jail under sentence of death."

"Truly. But the charge was false. The witnesses had lied."

"Do you remember who set him free?"

Ali Baba did not answer, but the expression of his eyes changed and by just the fraction of an inch he hung his head. He looked even better that way — more patriarchal than ever, blending savagery and humility.

"Do you remember the talk you and I had at the time I set him free? I knew who had done the murder he was to have been hanged for, didn't I?"

"It was no murder," the old man answered. "That man's father slew my father. It was justice."

"Nevertheless, you committed legal murder and I might have

hanged you. What says the Koran? Does it bid return evil for good? Does it say in the Koran that a captain of thieves has no honor and need not keep promises? What are you and I — friends or enemies?"

"Jimgrim, you know I am your friend! All my sons and grandsons are your friends. You know it!"

"That is what I have been told, but I have yet to see it proved."

"What can I do? I am an old man. Can I stay a massacre by wagging a gray beard in the *suk?*"

"That remains to be seen. I will tell you what I have done. I have a true friend in Jerusalem — a friend unto death. Also, those in authority in Jerusalem listen when I speak; to them I gave certain writings, sealed before I came away this morning. It was known how serious the situation is in this place; so it was agreed before I came away that if these boys de Crespigny and Jones should be killed — and of course I shall die with them in that case —"

"God forbid, Jimgrim!"

"Then that seal shall be broken, and because of what shall be found written the first to be hanged when reprisals begin shall be the sixteen sons and grandsons of Ali Baba ben Hamza. But the seal shall not be broken otherwise."

"Jimgrim, shall the sons be slain for the father's fault? That is not justice!"

"But concerning Ali Baba ben Hamza himself I made a different agreement. I said to that friend of mine in Jerusalem, who is a friend unto death: 'Ali Baba ben Hamza of El-Kalil,' said I, 'has said he is my friend, but hitherto has not yet proved it. At this time my life will be in Ali Baba's hands. If he keeps faith, well; but if not, attend thou to it, making sure meanwhile that the bayonet is sharp.' "

"A bayonet? That is no thing to mention between friends, Jimgrim!"

"No, but between enemies a final argument! I claim you as a friend. But if you are not willing, I shall know what to do next. It is doubtless written whether I am to die or not at this time; but the consequence of that is also written and the fruits of the tree of friendship, Ali Baba, are always sweeter than the excrements of enmity!"

"What can I do? I am old. And the fire is laid!"

"Can the old not keep their promises? Are the old ungrateful? Do the old, because they are old, forget their friends?"

"Nay, Jimgrim, on the contrary! But you must not be too hard with me."

The only thing about Grim that suggested militarism was his uniform. Shut your eyes to that and he was a business man driving a difficult bargain through to completion.

His iron eyes were steady, but not overbearing; they looked capable of dreaming as well as of discriminating, and faithful beyond measure.

His voice too, had a quality of sympathy, so that when he was most threatening he seemed most persuasive; and along with the good-tempered smile there was an ability that neither words nor attitude expressed, but that was unmistakable — to understand and allow for the other fellow's point of view.

"Is it hard, O captain of thieves, to keep faith?" he asked.

"To keep faith?" Ali Baba paused and stroked his beard. "That is all that God asks of any man. But it is often very difficult."

"I shall keep faith with you," Grim answered, smiling genially. "You owe me two lives — yours and your youngest son's."

"*Taib!* I will pay two lives. Nay, I will do better; I will repay fifteen for the two! Seventeen for two! Thy life, Jimgrim, and the two youngsters who have tried to rule here and these — even this Jew — the doctor at the mission hospital and the woman who helps him and your ten policemen; go all of you, and on my head be it if harm befalls you on the way! Go safely to Jerusalem. I give you leave to go!"

Grim laughed and leaned back to light a cigarette. It did not seem to me that he had won his case, but he acted as if there were almost nothing more to talk about, and Ali Baba's old brown eyes beamed with a new light.

"You have spoken, Ali Baba. Seventeen for two, and we'll call the account balanced. But the seventeen are yourself and your sixteen sons. And the account — that shall be the account I shall give of El-Kalil when I return to Jerusalem. My life and the life of all these is on the heads of Ali Baba and his sixteen sons and grandsons!"

"Allah!"

"Certainly," said Grim. "Let Allah witness!"

Then Ali Baba did a thing that hardly fitted into the modern frame. He stood up and I thought he was going to denounce us all, for he was trembling and his lips quivered.

His eyes were on Grim's, as steady as the Westerner's now, and for the space of half a minute he stood erect, seeming to grow in height as the dignity of olden days descended on him. Then, to my astonishment and Cohen's, he took Grim's hand and bowed and kissed it.

"It is written," he said. "Life for life. Friendship in return for friendship. In this affair thy way and mine are one, Jimgrim."

Grim nodded.

"I knew you'd do the right thing, Ali Baba. Now sit down again and let's discuss the details. When your sons and grandsons come what do you propose to say to them?"

"Let your heart speak to them with my tongue. Surely they will listen."

"What do you suggest?"

"Nay, I am in your hands. We seventeen are thieves, but we be honest men. With our lives and all that we have we are your servants until this affair is over."

"There hasn't got to be any affair," said Grim.

"Allah! I have seen a tree stand up against the hail, but the hail fell. I have seen the stones withstand the locusts, but the locusts came. Shall a river turn backwards in its course because Jimgrim bids it and seventeen thieves stand with him and say yes?"

"What is your story then, about you and your sixteen working miracles?"

"That is different. That is the fire-gift that we won by entering the tomb of Abraham."

"You've been using it by all accounts to stir up the city for a massacre of Jews."

"Truly. Fire begat fire in men's hearts. Shall it now put out the fire it lit?"

"Certainly."

"Allah! *Shi muhal!* You speak in riddles, Jimgrim!"

"Not I. Tell your sons and grandsons to repeat their miracle tonight. You'd better go along and help them. See that you all do your best. Only, instead of proclaiming that the massacre should be tonight, you must announce that tomorrow is the great night."

"And then?"

"Simply this — if a greater miracle than yours should take place tomorrow night, admit it. Confess that it is greater than yours and tell the crowd that it puts yours in the shade and makes the massacre inadvisable. In that way you'll save the situation and your own reputation as well. Will you do that?"

"*Taib.*"

As the old man gave his consent, reluctantly and only half-convinced, there came the stuttering ram-or-Goddamn-you roar of a motorcycle from the direction of Jerusalem. It stopped before the gate and in a minute a dusty British corporal stood saluting in the door.

"Dispatch for Captain de Crespigny!" he announced, in the matter-of-fact voice of a postman delivering the mail.

"I'll take it," answered Grim.

CHAPTER IV

"I feel like Pontius Pilate!"

Have you ever had an official dispatch passed to you to read, marked **SECRET**, that has been brought at sixty miles an hour by a grimy man on a motorcycle? It feels good, never mind what serious news it contains. Grim tore open the envelope, glanced at the single sheet and handed it to me; whereat I enjoyed all the sensations that attach themselves to unauthorized participation in events, all the thrills that come of reading tragic news — as if I were a spectator and not actor in a drama — and pride besides, because Cohen, of course, belonged to an inferior breed and might not read it.

"Any trouble on the way?" asked Grim.

"Nothing to speak of, sir. Fired at nine or ten times, but only one bullet through my tunic."

"Think you can get back all right?"

"Have a try, sir. Sixty mile an hour's a poor target. Gettin' dark too."

"Did you notice any signs of concerted action as you came along?"

"Can't say I did, sir. I was comin' that fast I didn't dare tike me eyes off the road. Them what fired at me was snipers."

Grim took the dispatch from me and handed it to Cohen. I had to recall deliberately that I liked Cohen. He read it in the manner of a dry-goods dealer opening the morning mail. What was worse, he read it aloud, destroying secrecy and ninety-nine percent of the Romance. What was the use of marking the thing **SECRET** in big black letters if it was to be treated like a newspaper, and in the presence, too, of the corporal who had risked his life to bring it? But the British are a strange race and Grim's way with some of their conventions was even more surprising.

" 'Jerusalem,' " read Aaron Cohen, " 'is fairly well in hand.' I suppose they mean by that the Moslems have quit knifin' for twenty minutes to go an' say their prayers! 'Several Jews and Moslems have been killed and a considerable number of both sides wounded.' You'll notice there's nothin' about British officers an' Sikhs. They ain't a side; they're on top! 'All gates have been closed and a guard set on the ramparts.' That's to keep Jews from escapin' while the Moslems do the dirty work! 'There is no reliable news from Hebron and it is therefore assumed that all is well there.' Say, ain't that English for you! 'The present moment is not favorable for sending detachments of troops, small or otherwise, to outlying places and it is therefore hoped that you will tide over the emergency without assistance.' Hey! I'm going to remember that! That's a pippin! Next creditor that writes me for something on account, I'm going to answer 'the present moment is not favorable for sending remittances, small or otherwise, to out o' town dealers, an' it is therefore hoped —' Oh, that's a lallopolooser! 'Word from you by bearer would be welcome, with any particulars that you think important.' Can't read his signature — looks like a G and an X and three Ws and a twiggly mark. Calls himself staff-major. I call him a genius! That man 'ud be worth any firm's money!"

He passed the letter back to Grim.

"Goin' to answer it? Let me answer it! I bet you I'll bring the Sikhs here in motor-trucks in two hours! What this Administration needs most is a course in business correspondence. Let me give him some particulars that I think important! I'll tell him!"

Grim, signing himself as "acting in temporary absence of the governor," wrote a few lines in a hurry and showed them to Cohen and me before he sealed them up.

Nothing unmanageable here yet, but when available a machine gun might be advisable for demonstration purposes. Expect to be able to carry on meanwhile without assistance, but advise that a company of Sikhs be sent as soon as possible.

James Schuyler Grim.

"You might be an out-o'-town drummer askin' the firm for samples!" was Cohen's comment on that. "What that firm needs is orders — 'Send hardware quick by express and men to demonstrate!'"

"That's all," said Grim, handing the corporal the envelope; and the man saluted and was gone. Two minutes later the bark of his exhaust began echoing off the stone walls and in a minute more our last link with civilized force had vanished out of hearing.

THEN, as the galloping explosions died in the distance the Governorate servant came in with the news that sixteen men were waiting at the gate. Grim told him to admit them and we went into the long hall to await their coming, sitting on a bench at the end like three kings on a throne, Grim, Cohen, and I, with Ali Baba standing like a lord high chancellor beside us.

They filed in one by one, mysterious and curious, peering this and that way in the deepening twilight, strangely heavy-footed in spite of a manner suggesting conspiracy, and not in the least at ease until Ali Baba spoke to them. I noticed that Grim was watching the old man narrowly; if a signal had passed I think he would have known it.

They were led by a giant — a bulky, bearded stalwart about forty years old, in a sheepskin coat that only half-concealed the heft of his shoulders. He wore a long knife in a sheath at his middle, but looked able to slay men, as Samson did, without it. The naked, hairy calf that showed for a moment through a slit in his saffron-colored smock was herculean with lumpy muscle, and he bowed to us with rather the air of a strong man favoring weaker brethren. But his smile — a streak of milk-white in the midst of glossy dark hair — was winning enough, for his brown eyes smiled too and were wide enough apart to look good-natured.

None of the rest was as tall as the first man, or as good-looking, although they were a magnificent gang and quite aware of it. They were used, those fellows, to the middle of the road and the deference the physically weaker pay to athletes who know their strength and value it. They seemed to own the earth they stood on.

There was a one-eyed man among them and one fellow much shorter than the rest, who made up for lack of inches by prodigious breadth and arms like a gorilla's, reaching nearly to his knees. Almost the last to enter I recognized our old friend Mahommed ben Hamza, grinning good-humoredly as ever, and swaggering with all the old "the world is mine oyster" manner that distinguished him at El-Kerak, when he held Grim's life and mine for a day or so in the hollow of his hand.

They were a strong-smelling company, but otherwise comforting to meet, since they were not to be enemies. There was a vague suggestion about them of a pack of hound-pups, ready to howl on a scent and tear their quarry in pieces, or to wag their tails and play; whichever might suit the huntsman's mood.

I dare say the lot of them weighed a ton and a half, and if you had boiled them down for fat you might have harvested a dozen pounds; but excepting that one characteristic of hard condition the only strong family resemblance that they all shared was a certain plastic serenity of forehead and breadth between the eyes.

"Show your respect to the gentlemen," Ali Baba ordered sternly, whereat they formed in double line across the hall and bowed with great dignity.

"Your father Ali Baba has a word to say to you all," announced Grim.

"We listen when he speaks," said the big man.

"Go on, Ali Baba."

"The Jews are not to die tonight. Jimgrim has spoken. Between us and Jimgrim is a covenant of blood. See ye to it that our honor is whole in this matter."

"Then the fire-gift? What of that?" asked the giant.

"Use ye the fire-gift as before. Use it this night. I come too, for Jimgrim has done me honor and set me free. But let it be known that it is not written for tonight. Perhaps tomorrow night, but not tonight by any means may Jews be killed."

There was a murmur of half-rebellion along both ranks, and an exchange of quick glances.

"Jimgrim is our brother," said the big man, "but who will listen now? They will smite us in the teeth and throw stones if we say now that what we said before was false! Moreover, they will draw their swords in spite of us."

I rather expected Grim would join in the argument at that point, but nothing of the kind.

"This is your gang, Ali Baba," was all he said, and sat well back, rather ostentatiously at ease. And the old man took the cue from him.

Never have I seen such fury — such sudden change from patriarchal dignity to blazing wrath; nor ever more surprising meekness in the face of it.

The old man raised both clenched fists and the very hairs of his beard seemed to stand apart and stiffen with the intensity of his frenzy.

"Shall I curse my sons?" he screamed. "Are these the men I got — the children of my loins that sneer in my face like idiots and answer Nay to my Yea? Is my old age a mockery that sixteen louts should dare know better than I? Leave me! I will marry wives and God will give me other sons! I will find me better sons in the *suk*! Is it not enough to be jailed by an infidel for the sake of a heretic Jew, that my own sons must come and mock my face and my gray hairs? Truly is Allah great and his judgment past discerning! All these years have I nurtured snakes, believing I was blessed in them. And so at last Allah clears my old eyes and shows me the poison in their teeth! Go! Go! I am a childless man! Better the dogs of the street than sons who mock their father! Go, I order you!"

But they did not go. Nor did they take his terrific reproof other than abjectly. They closed up and fawned on him, more than ever like hound-pups, looking more enormous than ever because of his age and comparative frailty — begging, imploring, coaxing him, calling him respectful names, making him promises that would have made Aladdin's eyes start, even after his experience with the wondrous lamp. Finally the biggest of them put their arms about him and bore him off in the midst of the sixteen, they still fawning and he protesting.

"So that settles that," said Grim, getting off the bench.

"Call that a settlement?" asked Cohen. "All you've done, as far as I can see, is to turn a lot of knifers loose on the town and nothin' gained but their own admission that they can't do a thing! They'll talk that old rooster over as soon as they get outside. Here it is dark already and a pogrom slated for tonight! Seems to me you're — Say, what do you figure you've done, anyway?"

But Grim is not given to explaining things much; he told me more than once he has a notion that discussing half-formed plans "lets off the pressure and drowns the spark." He looked at Cohen critically, but with that gleam of tolerant amusement that always takes the sting out of a remark:

"We've still got Aaron Cohen to fall back on," he answered quietly. "I'll bet with you, Aaron — my silver watch against your gold one that there won't be a throat cut in Hebron as long as you play the game!"

"Me? What game? Call this a game? Here, take the watch! I'll have no use for it this time tomorrow!"

"I'll trade with you. There, take mine. Now I'll bet with you the other way about. My gold watch against your silver one that you daren't play my game and pull this fat out of the fire!"

"May as well play your game as any man's!" laughed Cohen. "Are you thinkin' of issuing rain checks in case the knifing's put off till tomorrow?"

"I've offered to bet you that you daren't."

"Daren't what?"

"Play my game."

"Blind? All right, it's a bet! You show me the thing I daren't do!"

"I'll try!" Grim answered. "But I'd take ten cents for my option on your watch!"

De Crespigny and Jones came in together just then, laughing about some incident in the city; and the servant began laying the table for dinner with a brave effort to seem cheerful too, as if he hoped we might live to eat it. He was a wizened old city Arab, deeply pitted with smallpox marks, who had seen his share of trouble in Hebron and retained little except poverty and a huge capacity to doubt.

"The city's quiet," announced de Crespigny, as we started on the soup. "Either they're waiting for the men on the camels to bring back a report, or they've made up their minds to cut loose at midnight. There's no knowing which. I acted Dutch uncle to the head-men in the *mejliss* hall."

"How old was the youngest of them?" I asked him.

"Lord knows. Why? What difference does his age make? I told them they are responsible for good order in the city and that I'll hold their noses to it. The Jews made the most fuss; they're naturally scared. They demanded a curfew rule — everybody to be within doors after eight o'clock."

"Did you agree to that?" Grim asked — a shade sharply it seemed to me. He left off eating soup and waited for the answer.

"Didn't dare. Couldn't enforce it with ten policemen. So I pretended to give the idea a minute's consideration and then told 'em the head-men might make any ruling they liked and that at the first sign of disorder the head-men will be the ones who'll catch it! On top of that I told 'em I've decided not to send for troops as long as they behave themselves; thought that might explain away the fact that we can't get troops!"

"Good boy!" said Grim.

"I feel like Pontius Pilate!" laughed de Crespigny.

"He was better off; he had about a hundred men," said Jones. "All the same, you've done what he did. I was all through the city. You've jolly well got P. Pilate Esquire looking like a silver-plater cantering behind the crowd at the end of a season."

"Thanks!"

"What I mean is, I think you've kept on top. You were so jolly cool they think you've got a red ace up your sleeve."

"I'm hoping Grim has," said de Crespigny.

"Sure — I've got Cohen," answered Grim.

Cohen laid his spoon down and looked about him.

"Red ace? Me? Up anybody's sleeve? Say, quit your kiddin'!"

"All right. You're to do the kidding from now on."

"Kid myself, I suppose? Kid myself my stummik don't feel creepy each time there's a new noise in the street!"

"Yes, kid yourself. You're going to be an Arab after dinner."

"Well, give me a long knife then! Maybe I'll wave it an' preach a holy war an' lead all the Arabs in rings around the country until they get sore feet an' die o' homesickness? That's a better idea than any I've heard yet."

"You've got to lead Jews, not Arabs," Grim answered.

"Me? In this place? It can't be done. They're all Orthodox here. There isn't one of 'em would listen to me."

"We'll see," Grim answered and he would not say another word on the subject all through dinner.

It was not an easy meal. There were constant interruptions by mysterious men from the city who sought word with de Crespigny. Most of them were men who feared for their property in case of an outbreak of violence — for the Moslems loot pretty indiscriminately when the game begins, and he who has an enemy does well to watch him. But two or three of them were on the official list of spies and their reports were not reassuring.

However, we reached the stage of nuts and port wine without having been fired at through the window, which was something, and although there was an atmosphere of overhanging danger, not lessened by the smoky oil lamps and the shadows they cast on the wall, or by the dead silence of the street outside, broken only at intervals by the cough of the solitary sentry. I, for one, did not feel like a doomed man; and I suspected Cohen of feeling less afraid than he pretended. I think he was actually more nervous about what Grim had in store for him than creepy about Arab knives.

AFTER dinner the house was ransacked for Arab garments that would fit him, and in half an hour he was trigged out well enough to deceive any one. The Jewish are not unlike Arab features, in the dark especially, and there was less risk of his being detected than of my making some bad break that would give the three of us away; although by that time under Grim's tuition I had learned how to act an Arab part pretty well, provided I held my tongue.

Cohen could talk Arabic as easily as English, being a linguist like most Jews, as against my mere beginner's efforts. But Grim would not hear of leaving me behind. I am convinced that over and over again if he had left me out of things he could have accomplished his purpose more easily, but he has a sort of show-man instinct under his mask of indifference to side-issues, coupled to a most extravagant devotion to his friends.

I should say that his weakest point is that. He is inclined to run absurd risks to do a friend a favor, and takes a child's delight in springing a weird surprise on you, often for his purpose treating regulations and such encumbrances as if they never existed. And his friends are strictly of his own choosing. Nationality, creed, social standing, even morality, mean nothing to him when it comes to likes and dislikes, so that you often find yourself in strange company if you are lucky enough to stumble into his astonishing circle, as I did.

He and Cohen and I left the house by the front door — I with strict instructions to keep silent and much occupied with the difficulty of walking like a native. We went past the jail, where the man on duty did not recognize us, for he challenged gruffly and cautioned us to go home; then straight on down the empty street toward the city, where hardly a light hinted that more than twenty thousand people dwelt.

Parts of the ancient wall are standing, but there are no gates left and it was only as the street grew narrower and crooked that we knew we were within. There was no moon; so although the purple sky was powdered with blazing jewels, the shadows were black as pitch and it was more by watching the roof-line than the pavement that we found our way.

Now and then we passed under tunnels where ancient houses with six-foot-thick walls were built over the street; but those were generally lighted by dim oil lamps that flickered wanly, suggesting stealthy movements in the dark ten feet away.

It was clean enough underfoot, for those two boys had set at naught the Palestinian obsession for saving water that is as old as the tanks they preserve the rain in; but as the camel-load-wide street shut in on us, the smells of ancientry awoke, until we came to the ghetto and a stench like rotting fish put all other sensations for the moment out of mind.

You can get a suggestion of the same smell in New York in the small streets where the immigrants live awhile before they begin to absorb America.

There an iron lamp hung on a bracket and shed gold on the flanks and floor of a plain stone arch. There had been a great gate, for the hinges were there, but the gate was gone. Under the arch, beyond the farthest rays of lamplight was the night in its own home, blacker than the gloom of graveyards. There was not a sound or a suggestion of anything but mother-night, that you might lean against.

Grim led the way in. It felt like groping your way forward into a trap, for in spite of the insufferable silence — or because of it — there was a sensation after the first few yards of being watched by eyes you could not see and waited for by enemies who held their breath.

Twenty yards down a passage so narrow that you could touch

both sides at once without fully extending your arms Grim stopped and listened, and it was so dark that Cohen and I cannoned into him. Little by little then, you became aware of infinitely tiny dots of lights, where doors and shutters did not quite fit and once or twice of a footfall about as noisy as a cat's. There was teeming life behind the scenes, as awake and watchful as the jungle creatures that wander between the thickets when men go by.

Suddenly Grim began to call aloud in Hebrew, sending the mellow, rounded vowels booming along between the walls, but getting no response except the echo of his own voice. Three times he repeated what sounded like the same words and then turned back.

"Quick! Out of this! An Arab isn't safe here!"

By comparison the gloom of the street looked like daylight. We made for it like small boys afraid of graveyard ghosts.

"What did you say to them?" I asked and Cohen snickered.

"A verse from the Psalms in the original — 'Come, behold the works of the Lord. He maketh wars to cease unto the end of the earth; he breaketh the bow, and cutteth the spear in sunder; he burneth the chariot in the fire. Be still, and know that I am God. . . . The Lord of hosts is with us; the God of Jacob is our refuge.' "

"Now who's kiddin' himself?" asked Cohen. "You think they wouldn't sooner know the Sikhs were coming?"

"D'you know the history of your own people?" Grim answered. "There isn't a man in that ghetto who hasn't a sharp weapon of some kind. If they thought the Sikhs were on the way they'd very likely start something for the Sikhs to finish. That's crowd psychology. Get a number of people all in one place, hating one thing or afraid of one thing and any fool can stampede them into violence. Jews are fighters; don't forget it; if they weren't they'd have been exterminated long ago. If the Jews start anything tonight we're done for. That voice in the dark may make them think. Come on."

"Where are we going now?"

"To the Haram."

"Gee!"

There was no need to explain to Cohen what that meant and the deadly danger of it. Beneath the mosque in the Haram is the cave of Machpelah in which Abraham's bones are said to lie. The Arabs claim descent from Abraham in the line of Ishmael and Esau, and dwell lingeringly on the story of how both men lost their birthright, as they hold, unfairly; so now that they have the tables turned and own the tomb of the common ancestor, they take delight in keeping out the descendants of Jacob, and the death of a Jew caught in that place would be swift. Jews and other "infidels" with rare exceptions are allowed as far as the seventh step leading upward from the street, but not one inch nearer.

"Are we going inside?" asked Cohen.

"May as well."

"You've got your nerve!"

"We'll be safe if you've got yours."

Cohen did not answer and I would have given a lot to know just what was going on in his mind. If the prospect of entering that mosque thrilled me it must have meant vastly more to him, however broad his disrespect and loose his faith might be; for not a Jew had stood within stone-throw of the tomb of Abraham for nearly two thousand years, and all the Jews of the world, Orthodox or not, look back through the mists of time to Abraham at least as thoughtfully as does New England to the Pilgrim Fathers.

If he regarded Abraham as myth it was none the less an adventure to tread where no Jew had dared show himself for nineteen centuries; but I don't think he did, for you need not scratch the most free-thinking Jew particularly deep before you find a pride of ancestry as stiff as any man's. Cohen was not one of those "international" fire-brands that offend by denying race as well as creed, but a mighty decent fellow as the sequel showed.

Grim knew the way through the dark streets as a fox knows the rabbit-runs, and led without a moment's hesitation. His point of view was not so puzzling as Cohen's; he was like a knife that goes straight to the heart of things, as unconscious of resistance as a blade that is fine enough to slip between what heavier tools must press against and break.

Making our way continually southward, we threaded the quarter of the glass-blowers and the quarter of the water-skin makers, past endless shuttered stalls where lamp-light filtered dimly through the cracks in proof that the city was not asleep.

There was very little sound, but an atmosphere of tense expectancy. A few men were abroad, but they avoided us, slinking into shadows; for it is not wise to be recognized before the looting starts, lest an enemy denounce you afterwards.

The wise — and all Hebron prides itself on wisdom in affairs of lawlessness — were indoors, waiting. You felt as if the city held its breath.

When we drew near the Haram at last there was more life in evidence. It began with the street dogs that always leave their miserable offal-hunting to slink and be curious around the circle of men's doings. We had to kick them out of the way and were well saluted for our pains so that our arrival on the scene was hardly surreptitious.

Over the south entrance of the Haram a great iron lantern burned, and we could see the wall beyond it, of enormous, drafted, smooth-hewn blocks as old as history. Men were leaning against it and standing in groups, some of them holding lanterns and every one armed.

The men of Hebron, who pride themselves on fierceness, are at pains to look fierce when violence is cooking and the Arab costume lends itself to that. I think Cohen shuddered and I know I did.

Grim led straight on, as if he owed no explanation to the guardians of the place and did not expect to be called upon to give any.

But they stopped us at the entrance, an arch no wider than to admit two men abreast, and, because Grim was leading, hands that were neither too respectful nor over-gentle thrust him back, and fierce, excited faces were thrust close to his.

"Allah! Where are you coming? Who are you?"

"Heaven preserve you, brothers! Mahommed Hadad and two friends," Grim answered.

"What do you want?"

"To see the fire-gift."

"Whence do you come?"

"From Beersheba, where all men tell of the great happenings in El-Kalil."

"Ye come to spy on us!"

"Allah forbid!"

"Then to steal! Beersheba is a rain-washed bone; ye come to help loot El-Kalil and afterwards leave us to bear the blame for it!"

"*Shu halalk?* [What talk is this?] We be honest men. In the name of the Merciful, my brothers, we seek admittance."

"Are there Jews with you?"

"That is a strange jest! Who would bring a Jew to this place?"

"Nevertheless, let us see the others."

There were long, keen knives in their girdles. As Cohen and I raised our faces to be looked at we offered our throats temptingly and the goose-flesh rose all down my arms and thighs. Only a Jew can guess what Cohen felt; but a Jew looks exactly like an Arab when his face is framed in the *kufiyi*. Neither of us spoke. I stepped forward after Grim, trying to look as if I knew my rights in the matter, and Cohen followed me. In another second we were past the guard and mounting steps up which sudden death is the penalty for trespass.

CHAPTER V

"The mummery they call the fire-gift."

WHAT with darkness and the crowd and the fact that every one was busy with his own excitement we were safe enough until we reached the mosque door. The Haram is a big place with all manner of buildings opening off it — dwellings for dervishes for instance, a place for people known as saints, and a home for the guardians, who live separate from the saints and are said to have a different sort of morals altogether. The court was packed with men among whom we had to thread our way, and the steps leading up to the mosque were like a grandstand at a horse-race with barely foot-room left for one man at a time up the middle.

Directness seemed to be Grim's key. That as a fact is oftenest the one safe means of doing the forbidden thing. Your deferent, too cautious man is stopped and questioned, while the impudent fellow gets by and is gone before suspicion lights on him. But at the top of the steps we were met by the Sheikh of the mosque, who had eyes that could cut through the dark and a nose begotten out of criticism by mistrust; a lean, long-bearded man so steeped in sanctity and so alert for the least suspicion of a challenge to it that I don't believe a mouse could have got by uninvestigated. You could guess what he was the moment his eye fell on you and even by the dim light cast by an iron lantern on a chain above him his cold stare gave me the creeps.

It was baleful and made more so because he wore a turban in place of the usual Arab head-dress that frames and in that way modifies the harshness of a man's face. His beard accentuated rather than softened the pugnacious angle of his jaw, and if I am any judge of a man's temper his was like nitroglycerine, swift to get off the mark and to destroy.

But explosives, too, are forbidden things. If you mean to handle them the simplest way is best. Grim walked straight up to him.

"*Allah ybarik fik!* [God preserve you!] I bring news," he announced.

"Every alley-thief brings tales tonight!" the other answered. "Who are you? And who are these?"

"I bring word from Seyyid Omar, the Sheikh of the Dome of the Rock of El-Kudz [Jerusalem]."

"Allah! At this time?"

"What does necessity know of time? How many ears have you?"

It was pretty obvious that there were thirty pairs of ears straining to catch the conversation.

"You may follow me alone then."

But Grim knew better than to leave us two on the steps at the mercy of questioners. At the outer gate he had said we were from Beersheba in order to avoid the honor of an escort to the Sheikh. Now he claimed herald's honors for all three of us, for the same purpose of avoiding close attention.

"Three bore the news, not one," he answered.

"One is enough to tell it. I have not three sets of ears," snapped the Sheikh.

"Then you wish me to leave these two outside to gossip with the crowd?"

"Allah! What sort of discreet ones has Seyyid Omar chosen! Let them follow then."

So we fell in line behind him and passed through the curtains hung to shield from infidel eyes an interior that in the judgment of many Moslems is nearly as sacred as the shrine at Mecca.

Like so many of the Moslem sacred places it was once a church, built by the crusaders on the site of earlier splendor that the Romans wrecked — a lordly building, the lower courses of whose walls are all of ten-ton stones — a place laid out with true eye for proportion by men who had no doubt of what they did. For that has always been known as the veritable tomb of Abraham; no one has ever doubted it until these latter days of too much unbelief.

The higher critics will deny one of these days that Grant's body was ever buried in Grant's Tomb; but the lower critics, who are not amused by proof that twice two isn't four, will read of Grant and go and see and be convinced.

> And Abraham hearkened unto Ephron: and Abraham
> weighed unto Ephron the silver, which he had named in the
> audience of the sons of Heth, four hundred shekels of silver,
> current money with the merchant. And the field of Ephron,
> which was in Machpelah, which was before Mamre, the field,
> and the cave which was therein, and all the trees which were in
> the field, that were in all the borders round about, were made
> sure unto Abraham for a possession in the presence of the
> children of Heth, before all that went in at the gate of the city.
> And after this Abraham buried Sarah his wife in the cave of
> the field of Machpelah before Mamre: the same is Hebron in the
> land of Canaan. . . . Then Abraham died in a good old age and
> his sons Isaac and Ishmael buried him in the cave of Machpelah,

in the field of Ephron the son of Zohar the Hittite, which is
before Mamre; the field which Abraham purchased of the sons
of Heth: there was Abraham buried, and Sarah his wife.

You don't have to believe that straight-forward account, of
course, if you don't want to. And if you care to imagine that the
Jews and Arabs, who set so much store by Abraham, would ever
have forgotten the exact site of his burial-place, so that later
arrivals on the scene could not identify it, imagination, even of
that sort, does not have to be assessed for income tax. Go to it.

But you can't pass through those curtains into the mosque and
not believe. Not more than twenty non-Moslems in a thousand
years have been in there, and each has told the same tale of calm
conviction afterward. I heard Cohen catch his breath.

The whole place was full of men, who squatted on the priceless
rugs that cover every inch of a floor larger than some cathedrals
boast. We passed among them down the center aisle between two
cenotaphs that mark the graves of Isaac and Rebecca; for they
and Jacob and his wife as well, are buried in the same cave under
the mosque floor. But the Sheikh did not pause there; there were
too many who might listen, and the dim light from lamps that
hung on chains shone in their eyes as they watched us, and on
the hilts of swords, so that we seemed to be trespassing where
ghouls brewed wrath.

At the north end the Sheikh led into an octagonal-shaped cha-
pel, with the cenotaphs of Abraham and Sarah draped with green
and crimson in the midst; and why that place was deserted just at
that time was a mystery, for there was no barrier to exclude any
one. Not a soul moved in there; none whispered in the shadows.
The Sheikh and we three squatted down on a Turkoman rug
above Abraham's bones and faced one another unlistened to,
unseen.

"What now?" said the Sheikh. "Be quick with your message.
This is no time for gossip. I have my responsibilities."

As Cohen had remarked, Grim had his nerve with him. Face to
face with that explosive-minded Sheikh he came straight to the
point. I have seen lion-tamers act the same way; they don't pretty-
pussy the beast through the bars, but go right in and seize the
upper hand.

"Seyyid Omar of El-Kudz [Jerusalem], Sheikh of the Dome of
the Rock, demands to know why you dare permit this place to be
polluted by the mummery they call the fire-gift! All the City is talking of it."

"Allah! Am I dreaming? Who are you that dare speak such insolence to me?"

"Seyyid Omar's messenger."

"Show me a writing from him."

Grim shook his head and sneered.

"It is from you that there must be a writing. I come with two witnesses to hear me ask the question and to prove that I report your answer truly. Shall I ask a second time?"

THE Sheikh glared back and bit his beard, tortured I thought, between indignation and fear. I guessed Grim was on pretty safe ground now, for he knew Sheikh Seyyid Omar of El-Kudz intimately, and to my knowledge had done him a greater service than could ever be lightly overlooked; he was truly delivering a message from him for aught I knew; more improbable things have happened. True message or not, he waited with the air of a man who represents high authority.

"What business is it of Seyyid Omar's? Let him mind his own mosque!"

"It is his judgment," Grim answered, "that this place is lapsing into disrepute. If that is true it is his duty to accuse you. If the fault is not yours, although the charge is true, it is his purpose to help you remedy the matter."

"It is not my fault."

"But the charge is true?"

"Allah pity us, it is true! But how can Seyyid Omar help — a fat man with both hands full of troubles of his own?"

"He has sent us three."

"If you were three angels with the trumpet of Gabriel I fail to see how you could set matters straight. There are seventeen thieves of El-Kalil who have tricked me and won the upper hand. May the curse of the Most High break their bones forever!"

"Who are they?"

"Ali Baba ben Hamza and his brood of rascals."

"I have heard of them. Such ignorant men can surely never get the better of us."

"They have it! Listen. That old dog Ali Baba ben Hamza came to me and said: 'I am old and my sins weigh heavy on me. I saw a vision in the night. A spirit appeared to me and said I must pray all night at the tomb of Abraham, I and my sixteen sons, together with none watching. So I may obtain mercy and my sons shall have new hearts.' That was fair speaking, was it not? Who am I that I should stand between a man and Allah's mercy? But they are thieves, those seventeen, and the charge of this mosque is mine; so I would not lock them in the place alone, as they desired. I and another entered with them on a certain night and locked the door."

"Leaving no guard outside?" asked Grim.

"Leaving seven men outside, whose orders were to stay awake. But they slept. When the door was locked those seventeen devils took me and the man who was with me, and laid cloths over our faces, having first saturated the cloths with a drug they had stolen from the hospital. I know that, because the foreign doctor made complaint afterwards that his drugs had been stolen. So I and the man who was with me also slept, I do not know how long. When we awoke we were deathly sick and vomited."

"Where were the seventeen thieves by that time?" Grim asked him, for the Sheikh seemed too disturbed by the memory to go on with the tale.

"They were here, where we sit now. But I did not go in to them at once. They had laid me and the man who was with me in the northern porch not far from the cenotaphs of Jacob and his wife, and to reach them I had to pass by the entrance to the cave that has been sealed up these eight hundred years. Then I made a terrible discovery. Allah! But my eyes popped out of my head with unbelief! Yet it was so. The masonry had been broken through! They had been down into the tomb of Abraham!"

"Did you go and see what they had done down there?" Grim asked.

"*Shi biwakkif!* [Who could think of such a thing!] Allah! I did not dare! Eight hundred years ago a Turkish prince defied the guardians of the mosque and entered the tomb alone. He came groping his way out with eyesight gone, and could never tell what befell him, for his speech was also taken. After that the opening was sealed. Nay, I did not dare go. Who knows what spirits dwell in that great cave? But when my fear was a little overcome and wrath succeeded it I came in here to see what manner of curse had fallen on those seventeen men. They were breathing fire! As I sit here and Allah is my witness, they were breathing flame! It shot forth from their mouths as I stood and watched them!"

"And the man who was with you? What did he do all this time?"

"He came and stood beside me and saw all that I saw and bore witness. I took courage then, having another with me, and together we approached Ali Baba, who sat where you sit, and I demanded what it all might mean. The old thief — the old trespasser — the old damned rake answered that while he and his sons prayed there came an angel, who touched with his fingers the masonry that closed the entrance to the cave, so that it fell."

"How did he account for your not seeing this?" asked Grim.

"He said that, the vision not being intended for me, the presence of the angel overpowered me and the man who was with me and we swooned. I accused him of having drugged us, but he answered that we must have dreamed that. The dog of a thief!"

"Well, go on. What next?"

"He said that the angel beckoned and he and his sixteen rascals followed into the tomb of Abraham, where a spirit came and breathed on them and they all received the gift of fire. In proof of it every one of the sixteen eggs of Satan belched fire from his mouth as the father of thieving spoke.

"You should have summoned your seven men, and have sent them for others, and have had Ali Baba and his thieves jailed for sacrilege," said Grim.

"But I tell you the seven men slept! I opened the door and shouted for them, but none came; and Ali Baba and his sixteen dogs pushed past me through the door and were gone! So after we had locked the door again I and the other man who was with me took counsel together and I was for sending for the Governor of Hebron; but he said that would be to make a public scandal, which it were well to avoid.

"He said that the Moslems of Hebron would not be pleased with us if it were known that we had let ourselves be tricked in such a matter and that they would be yet less pleased with us if we should appeal to foreigners. Moreover, he confessed himself afraid. He said that after all the story of the angel might be true and that if we denied it there might be a tumult. There are many wild fools in El-Kalil!"

"But you, not he, are the Sheikh of the mosque," said Grim.

"Truly. Yet he refused to follow the course I favored. He vowed that he would tell what he had seen with his own eyes and no more: to wit, the broken masonry and seventeen men all breathing fire in this place where we sit. He insisted that the wisest course for both of us would be to say nothing and to wait and see what Ali Baba and his sons might have to say first; to that course he was willing to agree.

"There is wisdom in silence; so he and I carried in cement and replaced the broken masonry with great care, agreeing to tell no word of it to any man until circumstances should reveal to us the right course. And the day following he ran away, Allah knows whither; so I am all alone to bear the brunt of this matter. Allah send a poor man wisdom that I may avoid disgrace!"

"Well — what account has Ali Baba given of it?"

"Have you not heard? He and his brood go belching Hell-fire through the streets, saying they went into the cave and have a gift of prophecy. When men came to see the entrance of the cave and found it sealed up, that old father of lies declared that one angel had broken the masonry, and afterwards another came and closed it. They could see that the cement was fresh and the stones slightly disarranged and that convinced them! Do you realize my predicament? My choice lay between confession that I had not guarded the cave faithfully, or saying nothing. I have said nothing. I continue to say nothing. Let Allah speak, or the spirit of Abraham, for I am dumb!"

"I find that you have been unwise," said Grim after a minute's pause; and for half a minute after that the Sheikh battled with his own priestly pride. For many and many a year he had been fault-finder-in-chief in Hebron, and the licensed critic of others seldom suffers judgment doucely. However, he swallowed the verdict, Grim watching him as if a chemical experiment were taking place in a test-tube.

"But not unfaithful," Grim added, when the right second seemed to have come to drop that new ingredient into the mixture of emotions.

The Sheikh's eyes that had been blazing grew as grateful as a dog's.

"Moreover, I find that the wisdom of your subsequent silence offsets the former foolishness and I shall say so to Seyyid Omar when I go back to El-Kudz."

"*Istarfrallah!* [I beg God's pardon!]"

"In silence there is dignity, and out of dignity may come deliverance," said Grim.

"*Inshallah!* [If God wills!]"

"Those seventeen thieves are not men of keen intellect, are they?" Grim asked him suddenly.

"Allah! They are rogues with the brains of foxes — no better and no less."

"How should they have thought of such a scheme as this?"

"*Shi ajib.* [It is a strange thing.] Who can fathom it?"

"There must be a brain behind them."

"Perhaps the brain of Satan! Who knows?"

"Think!" said Grim. "Is there any foreigner in Hebron who might have put them up to it?"

"I know of none."

"Has there been no stranger here, who perhaps took a particular interest in the entrance to the cave?"

"Ah! There was one, yes — about a month ago. But he was a dervish out of Egypt — a mere fanatic — a fool who did tricks with coins and eggs to amuse folk and begged his living."

"Where is he now?" asked Grim.

"They say he lives in a cave near Abraham's Oak."

"You say a mere mountebank?"

"No better."

Grim proceeded to dismiss that subject as beneath consideration. If I had dared air my Arabic I would have urged him to follow it up further and by the look in Cohen's eye he felt the same about it; but the most that either of us dared do was to sit still and call as little attention to ourselves as possible. Nothing but the fact that Grim had forced the Sheikh on the defensive from the start was preserving us from being questioned in a way that would have exposed me certainly, and Cohen probably.

"And this fire-gift — they are going to display it now?" asked Grim, as if he did not know.

"Aye, now. And I, who am Sheikh of this mosque, must eat humility and watch them. Truly are the ways of Allah past discerning. Verily dust is dust."

"Amen!" said Grim. "But did you never see a vision? May the Sheikh of a mosque such as this not talk with spirits now and then?"

The Sheikh stared back at him with his jaw down. You could have put anything into his mouth that you cared to and he wouldn't have known it; the suggestion had hit home.

"If seventeen thieves can see an angel," Grim went on, as if propounding a conundrum, "how many can the Sheikh of this mosque see?"

"But the fire-gift? These men show a miracle. How to answer that?"

"With another."

"But — but — I am no mountebank. I can do no tricks with fire."

"New tricks would do no good without a prophecy," said Grim. "In a matter of prophecy, whose word would be listened to, yours or theirs?"

"*Inshallah,* mine!"

"And which is wiser: to confound your adversary with his own arguments, or yours?"

"With his. Surely with his, for then he has no retort."

"So then — these seventeen thieves say that the fire-gift came out of the tomb of Abraham. If you were to say that because they are thieves the fire-gift must return again; if you were to say that an angel had appeared to you and told you that, would not all Hebron listen?"

"It might be. But Ali Baba and his sixteen sons have preached a killing of the Jews. The swords of El-Kalil are sharpened. They are ready to begin."

"Yes, and if they do begin all Hebron will say afterwards that the fire-gift and the prophecy were true. Ali Baba will be reckoned a true prophet and you will have a competitor on your hands."

"Truly."

"Therefore the massacre must not begin. Therefore you must stand up in the mosque now, and say you have seen a vision."

"But if I tell them there must be no massacre they will hurry all the faster to begin it; for that is the way of the men of El-Kalil."

"Not if you promise the chance of a greater miracle."

"But what then? What shall I promise?"

"Say that the angel said to you, 'These seventeen men are thieves and stole the fire-gift. Therefore there is a condition made. Not one Jew must be slain until the Jews shall have their chance to bring the fire-gift back. If they do bring it back, well; they are reprieved. They have one day and night in which to do it, and if a Jew is slain meanwhile there will be a vengeance on El-Kalil such as never yet befell — a vengeance of wrath and death and ruin. But if the Jews shall fail to bring it back, let them take the consequences!' "

"These are dark words," said the Sheikh.

"They are wise words."

"Inshallah, the plan can do no harm. If the Jews can make no miracle, at least I shall have taken something of the influence away from Ali Baba. This massacre is not good; delay might prevent it and avoid the punishment the British would mete out afterwards. Good. I will stand in the mosque and say I have seen a vision!"

"Better do it now," said Grim. "It's getting late."

"Come ye, and sit in the mosque then, and listen!"

CHAPTER VI

Fortune favors the man who favors fortune.

VIEWED in the light of what subsequently happened it seems possible that Grim's whole plan might have ended in disaster, if at that critical moment circumstances out of his control had not shaped themselves to aid him. But after a deal of blundering and being blundered up and down the world's by-ways I have learned and know by heart now these two fundamentals: there is nothing so unprofitable as to speculate in terms of "might have been;" and fortune favors the man who favors fortune.

That last sounds like heresy, or one of those Delphic deliveries that can be read in any of a dozen ways. Well, so it is and so it can be. All accepted doctrine was heresy at some time; and since no two men are quite alike, no two interpretations match exactly. If you call fortune "luck," luck is a chancy entity, and you will govern yourself and be governed accordingly.

I have heard of Washington and Lincoln both described as lucky, yet take leave to doubt that either of them gave a fig for luck. Both men, according to my reading of events, were fortunate. Fortune is fair and absolute and kind and generous. They favored her and so she favored them. In all the intimate and various relations that I had with Grim he never once referred to luck in terms of envy or esteem, but very often did describe himself as fortunate. Luck was the other fellow's talisman — the enemy's; fortune, his.

When luck came his way he laughed and mistrusted it. On the other hand, when fortune met him in the way he seemed to know the lady at the first glance, which is a rather rare advantage and accounts, I suspect, for some men being senators while others clean the streets.

So, as the old tale-craftsmen used to phrase it in the days when men thought more and squandered less, it fortuned that those camel-men returned from Jerusalem while we were entering the Mosque of Abraham. They went first to the Governorate and it fortuned that de Crespigny advised them to keep the camels until morning for their better convenience in spreading the news. So they lost no time; and being Hebron men with an inborn understanding of the city's ways, they came straight to the Haram where they felt sure in a time of excitement of finding the greatest possible number of men assembled in one place.

They gave their news to the crowd outside and entered the mosque by the south door exactly at the moment when the Sheikh at the opposite end turned into the center aisle with his mind made up to ascend the pulpit and tell his story of having seen a vision.

So he waited until they had done unburdening themselves of tidings to the swarm that closed around them. An Arab would rather have news to tell than a bellyful, and he likes his meal at that; so the two men made quite a ceremony of it, neither of them feeling inconvenienced or disappointed by being the center of attention. You could hear every word as they made the most of brief importance; and they were not unconscious of the obligation they owed to be accurate, since it was no small honor to have been selected to be witnesses of grave events.

"The story of a massacre by Jews is not true. There has been fighting. The Jews started it by insulting Moslems. A few were killed. Many hundred of both sides have been wounded. But the troops are now in control. There are barriers across the streets. The city gates are shut. We saw the administrator and he assigned an officer to show us all we cared to see. The Moslem holy places are intact and guarded by British troops.

"We asked the administrator whether troops would be sent to Hebron and he said no, there was no need; but we think that is because there are no troops that can be spared. He said there are plenty of troops, but we did not believe him; there are enough to hold the City quiet but no more. It is our belief that there is no further danger of the Jews massacring Moslems in Jerusalem. Moreover, that administrator is a man to be reckoned with, with whose wrath it is not wisdom to take chances."

Grim began whispering to the Sheikh, who was stroking that sacerdotal beard of his in a conflict of emotions. It was a serious enough crisis in his affairs, for if he should give the wrong advice or make the unacceptable statement at that moment it was likely his own influence would be gone forever, and possibly the salaried position with it.

It was by Grim's urging that he mounted the ancient pulpit — a marvel of a thing, made of Cedar of Lebanon for a Christian bishop in crusader times.

We three squatted in darkness by the wall and watched him. I thought Grim looked worried. The worst kind of fool on earth and the likeliest to make irreparable blunders is the man who is thinking of his own position first, as that Sheikh was undoubtedly. He stood stroking his beard, sharp-eyed and hook-nosed as

The Seventeen Thieves of El-Kalil

an eagle, peering this and that way into all the shadows until the crowd became aware of him and spread itself to squat down on the mats to listen to him.

There is a peculiar democracy about the Moslem faith. Their whole law is religious, and they recognize no other legislation if they can help it. Once let him convince them that a given course is indicated in the Koran and any one can do almost as he likes with them. Any one can get a hearing; but they usually concede to their appointed officials the right to speak first, after which they are ready to argue endlessly, so that the first speaker does well to be primed with something solid that can stand the devastating discussion which is sure to follow.

The Sheikh was an old hand at making an impression. He let the silence settle down and grow intense before he spoke and then began acridly with an accusation.

"Ye listen to this and that man and the latest comer has your ear. The wind brings dust and ye call that news. A camel coughs in the *suk,* and ye say a prophet speaks. The breath of your mouthings fills the air like bad smells from a dung-heap, and ye call that wisdom. Ye pray, and to what end? That your vain imaginings may take form. Ye ask Allah, the all-wise, to change the universe to suit your foolishness, imagining that fools are competent to give advice to the Creator. It is written that the fool shall rue his folly, and the headstrong man shall dread the day of reckoning!"

He had their attention pretty thoroughly by that time, for nothing takes hold of the mind of a crowd so quickly as a string of platitudes, especially when they sting. Flattery is the weapon for the demagogue who seeks to stir a crowd to action; if he would rather hold them and win delay, a dozen acid generalities about their sins work wonders. But those are rules that all the mob-leaders understand.

"While ye looked for wisdom in the cesspools," he went on scornfully, "I turned to the Book. And while I read and prayed there came an angel and I saw a vision — here in this place where the footstep of the Prophet is imprinted in the stone on which he stood. Here above the tomb of Abraham I saw a true vision!"

There was silence for a moment in which you could hear one man cracking the joints of his toes nervously. Then a voice cried out that Allah is all-powerful, and one after another repeated it until they were all chanting the first principles of Moslem faith, whose repetition seems to prepare them to believe anything — do anything — submit to anything.

"God is God. There is no God but God. Mahommed is his prophet."

The great roof hummed with the chant for about two minutes, until it suddenly occurred to them that they had not heard the details of the vision yet, and they ceased as suddenly as the frogs cease piping when a stone is thrown into the pond.

"The angel who appeared to me was angry. I was afraid and my bones shook," the man in the pulpit snarled; for he was one of those who take religion without sugar and grow nasal as they speak of sacred things. "He told me that the fire that came forth from the tomb of Abraham is in the hands of thieves, who took it in order to stir strife against the Jews. Because they are thieves," said he, "they are unfit to return it; yet unless it be returned there will be a judgment on El-Kalil. So I laid my forehead on the floor and prayed to know by whose hand that fire may be returned, that the city may be saved from judgment. And he said, 'Lo: against the Jews it was taken. Therefore let the Jews return it and they shall save themselves. For a day and a night let them have time given them; and if they return it, well, they have saved themselves and are reprieved. For a day and a night let not a Jew in El-Kalil be slain. But if they do not return it, then shall their blood be on their own heads.'

"Then the angel left me and my strength returned so that the bones of my legs no longer shook; but for a little while my eyes were still dazed by the brightness, so that I could neither see nor grope my way. After certain minutes my sight came again and then I lost no time, but came hither; and now ye know the vision I have seen. I have not kept it secret from you. As for him who chooses not to listen, let his blood be on his head. My hands are henceforth clean in this matter."

"For a leader he's easily led," Grim whispered. "But for a liar he's not half bad. Now if Ali Baba ben Hamza has only done his end of the talking too, we ought to manage nicely. Drat him! Is he going to read to them? This session'll last all night if we don't look out."

THE Sheikh had opened a great illuminated copy of the Koran and was turning over the pages in search of some passage that would suit the occasion. But just as he began to roll his tongue around the opening syllables the south door opened and a man called into the mosque that the fire-gift was about beginning.

That was too much for the congregation. It was like announcing to a Sunday school that the circus was outside. Perhaps they would have sat still if the vision he had told of had not been related to the fire-gift. As it was they rose like one man and surged through the door to see this thing again that caused so much concern among the angels. We followed at the tail of the procession.

But it was hopeless to try to see from the steps. The men in front had been forced forward by those behind, who now blocked the door and stood jammed like herrings, while the men below tried to regain the vantage of the steps for a better view.

"Follow me!" said Grim suddenly and led us at a run back into the mosque, where we overtook the Sheikh at the north end and were just in time to get out through a side door after him before he locked it. Grim seemed to know the way perfectly, for he did not hesitate but led across a small court, and making use of a buttress in a corner climbed up on a wall built of gigantic blocks of dressed stone. It was three feet wide on top, and at the end of thirty yards or so it gave us a perfect view of the court of the Haram and the crowd that milled below.

That was a sight worth seeing, for the fitful light of two oil lanterns shone on a sea of savage faces and, except where an occasional lantern swung in a man's hand, the rest was all black shadow. It was as if the night had a thousand heads. Not one body was visible from where we stood. Countless faces swam in a sea of darkness. And presently they sang, as the men of El-Kalil have always done when more than a dozen of them get together.

It would have been effective singing anywhere, at any time. The tune was as old as El-Kalil, which was a city in the time of Abraham. One man sang the words of a song that had no rhyme, but only a wavering, varying meter; and whenever they thought he had trolled out enough of it they suddenly thundered out the same refrain, bowing their heads together like pouter-pigeons making love. And the least apparent thing was its absurdity. It was the heart of El-Kalil responding to the voice of ages plucking at the strings of memory and stirring the racial passion.

> And he [Ishmael] will be a wild man; his hand will be against every man, and every man's hand against him; and he shall dwell in the presence of his brethren.

That night I almost understood the ancient curse, or blessing — whichever it is — that has lived with the Arabs since Hagar, their first mother, was driven forth into the desert to face the fruits of jealousy alone. You can't explain the Arab in any other way. In his heart and generally near enough the surface is the sense of being heir to the wrongs of ages, and a sort of joy in outlawry as birth-right. It lives in his scant music, in the primitive, few measures of his dance, in his poetry, in his nomadic instinct; and it comes to the surface at the least excuse or without any, whenever a crowd gathers — simple, savage, manly, not easy to condemn.

There are fields, there are olives, there are grapes in El-Kalil."
ALLAH! OH! IL-ALLAH!"
There are mountains all about her where the black goats graze, where the herdsmen keep the cattle, where the barley laughs and rustles in the wind."
ALLAH! OH! IL-ALLAH!
There are springs of lovely water never-failing, and the almond and the *mishmish* bloom and fruit in El-Kalil.
ALLAH! OH! IL-ALLAH!
In a valley on a mountain like a virgin's bosom, fair and full of scent is El-Kalil.
ALLAH! OH! IL-ALLAH!
Up among the stars, the colored stars of heaven, much desired of other men, the city of our fathers, the city of Er-Rahman, the home of Ali Bakka, the place of the Kashkala, the tomb, the tomb of Jesse, the place of Forty Martyrs, the delight of all the saints is El-Kalil.
ALLAH! OH! IL-ALLAH!
Like her flowers, like the soft eyes of her daughters, like her honey, like the bloom upon her bosom in the morning is the glass of El-Kalil.
ALLAH! OH! IL-ALLAH!
And the swords of El-Kalil, the keen swords, the strong swords swinging in her son's hands — mighty are the swords of El-Kalil!
ALLAH! OH! IL-ALLAH!

The song was beginning to get dangerous. The desert centuries have taught the Arab that beauty and peace are but oases in the midst of cruelty; and just as he must leave the place of meditative calm to strive against hot winds and drought and bitterness before he can rest again, so his mind moves swiftly from delight in beauty to the thought of cruelty and death.

But a path was cleft suddenly down the midst of the sea of faces like the winding, narrow channel of black water when the ice breaks up in Spring; and down the middle of that came Ali Baba, prancing with his skirts tucked up and followed by his sixteen sons. Each one of them breathed orange-colored flame out of his mouth at intervals and danced between-whiles, swaying to right and left to belch fire at the crowd and frighten them.

It was weird — astonishingly well-staged. You could only see arms, legs, bodies for a moment when the fire flashed; then the velvet darkness of the night between walls swallowed all but faces that milled and surged as if borne on an inky river.

The seventeen thieves passed swiftly, too well-versed in the lore of trickery to give spectators time for keen inspection. They vanished through the outer gate into the night and the gap closed up behind them. Then the song began again, starting this time on the theme of blood and sacrifice. Swords began to leap out and a roar went up from the outer circles of the throng that gained in volume as infection grew, and at the end of about two minutes some one with a bull's voice thundered:

"Now for the Jews! In the name of Allah, kill the Jews!"

"To the sword with them in the name of Allah!" another yelled from the darkness just below us. And a pause followed, of sudden, utter silence. They were wondering. They had heard strange things that night and seen strange sights. The yeast of uncertainty was working.

Then Grim took a long chance. We were thirty feet above them out of reach and there were no stones they could have flung; but the risk was infinitely greater than that. If he failed to touch the right chord of emotion; if he said the wrong word or overplayed the right appeal; if one ill-considered phrase should seize their fancy and fire imagination to take flight in violence, or one careless hint spur resentment, they would surge out of the Haram like a flood. The Governorate would be the first point of attack; then the Jews; then, perhaps, when the looting was over there would be a march on Jerusalem and a mess midway to the tune of stuttering machine guns.

Grim's voice broke the silence like a prophet's; for you have to speak in measured cadence if you hope to make an impress on the Moslem mind when the wild man heritage is uppermost and fierce emotion sways him. They could see only the outline of his figure against the deep purple setting of the stars and in those Arab clothes he looked enough dignified to be a true seer. Cohen and I drew away from him to give him the full dramatic force of loneliness.

"Brothers! The bones of Abraham lie under us. It is written that 'They plotted, but Allah plotted and of plotters Allah is the best.' When Abraham went forth to war with kings, he waited for the word that should send him forth, and he took no share of the plunder, lest one should say an enemy and not Allah had enriched him. Who are ye but sons of Abraham?

"We have heard and seen strange things this night," continued Grim. "And it is written, 'When ye prided yourselves on your numbers it availed you nothing.' Is it wiser to be headstrong at the bidding of the rash or to wait for the appointed time and see? For all is written. 'Who shall set forward by an hour the courses of the stars or change the contour of the hills or postpone judgment?' *Allah ykun maak!* [God be with you!]"

He had struck the right note. He had them. A murmur of low voices answered him and though the words were hardly audible the purport was plain; it was something about Almightiness and Allah. You can not separate the Moslem from his fatalism and it works either way, making him fierce or meek according to circumstance and the method of appeal. Unless some unexpected incident should occur to change their mood again it was likely they would cut no throats that night.

But the risk entailed by lingering another minute on the scene would have been deadly. Questions and answers might have produced the very spark needed to fire them to fanatical zeal again. The cue was to disappear at once, leaving the dramatic effect at its height and there was only one way to do that.

Black shadow lay behind us and beneath. I could just make out a suggestion of something solid that might be a roof and might not, but there was no time for investigation. Grim seemed to step off the wall into nothing and the darkness swallowed him. I jumped and Cohen lay down on the wall and rolled off, clinging to the edge with both hands.

THAT wasn't a roof. Grim had landed feet-foremost on a lower wall that met ours at right angles and it was the shadow cast by that that looked like something solid. I fell for a life-time, wondering what death would be like when the earth should rise at last and meet me, and was disgusted — disappointed — maddened when the end came.

They cover up the water as a rule in Hebron ; but that stone tank was open and the green scum floated on it inches thick. There were long green slimy weeds that clung and got into your mouth and eyes and if the water of the Styx tastes worse than that I'd rather live in this world for a while yet.

But it was not all bitterness. There was Cohen. He had to jump, too; and when I had scrambled out I told him all about it and then waited until his fingers lost their hold on the wall and he came catapulting down for his green bath just as I had done; and he liked it even less. He made remarks in Yiddish that I couldn't understand and refused to apologize for having splashed me.

Then Grim came, cool and dry, having found some goat's stairway down to *terra firma.*

"Both alive?" he asked. "Well — what's the general impression? What do you think of it all?"

"Me?" said Cohen. "Think? God damn it all! I've got to follow them thieves down into Abraham's cave or bust with curiosity!"

"You'll bust then, for it can't be done!" said Grim.

CHAPTER VII

"Your friends, Jimgrim, don't forget it!"

WE HURRIED back to the Governorate as straight as you can go through the mazy streets of Hebron and found Jones asleep in his boots on the bench at the end of the hall. De Crespigny was dozing on the window-seat in the sitting-room, and made a show of being angry with Jones for not having gone to bed.

"Fat lot of use you'll be this time tomorrow!"

"Do you see me bedded down, while you face the music alone?" Jones answered testily.

"Seems to me I've heard somewhere of juniors obeying orders!"

"You told me to go and get some sleep. I did."

Grim recounted what had happened at the Haram, while de Crespigny mixed drinks and a sleepy Arab servant stripped Cohen and me of our slimy wet garments.

"So you can both sleep safely until morning," Grim assured them. "Tell you what: I shan't need Cohen until after breakfast. Let him sleep in the hall. He'll give the alarm if a mouse breaks in. He's nervous."

"Noivous? Me? After breakin' into a mosque an' doin' a Hippodrome high-divin' stunt into a dark tank? You mean noivy!"

"I mean sleep," said Grim. "There's a bellyful in store for you tomorrow. Thought I'd try you out this evening. You've made good. Tomorrow you win the game for us."

"If you're countin' on me to make a home run I'll start now!" said Cohen. "Give me one o' them camels and I'll make it quicker! Mnyum-m! Never knew a hot cocktail could sink without makin' you sick. Does the business, too. Saves ice. Start a new fashion if I live through this. Warm drinks! Sure, give me another one!"

"Can you spare me one policeman, Crep?"

"Which?"

"Any one at all who knows Abraham's Oak and the caves thereabouts," Grim answered.

"Righto! I'll dig you out a man."

"Tell him to bring handcuffs."

"When d'you want him?"

"Now. I've got to move quickly. Our side-show's scheduled for tomorrow night and we don't want a rival act playing the same pitch. We've got to pull up that fire-gift by the roots. Besides, we need the makings. Some of the notables are likely to call on you at dawn, 'Crep, and tell you their version of tonight's events. If I were you I'd take the line that you'll permit crowds in the streets leading to the Haram tomorrow night to see the Jews return the fire-gift; but make them swear by their beards there shall be no bloodshed if the Jews don't disappoint them. Take their pledge in writing for it. Then how would it be if you offered to grace the ceremony with your official presence?"

"Good. That'll do to remind 'em of what they've promised. But Lord help us if you fail, Grim! Are you sure of the Jews?"

"That's Cohen's end."

"Say, see here," put in Cohen, "I've told you more'n once these Jews are Orthodox. They'd no more listen to me than if I was a Piute Indian. They'd sooner listen to an Indian!"

"Go to sleep on the bench and dream of a way of persuading them," Grim suggested pleasantly. "Policeman ready, Crep?"

The servant had found me dry clothes belonging to the estate of an Arab who had been hanged for triple murder a couple of weeks before, and Grim and I left by the front door again with the policeman shouldering a loaded rifle just behind us.

This time instead of turning toward the city we went almost to the opposite direction, between orchard walls, by a path so stony that you tripped at every second step. The policeman's steel-capped boots struck sparks behind us and the noise we made set little foxes scampering, then brought them back again to leap on the wall and look. Surely all nature wonders at the clumsiness of man.

WE WERE in open country at the end of half a mile, but that brought us small advantage, for the tilled hillsides to left and right of us were so much blackness, and how in the world Grim proposed to find any given cave, or the man who hid in it, was more than I could guess. You could see dim ghosts that were thousand-year-old olive-trees and goblins that were limestone rocks. Little owls screamed mockery from almost arm's length and one or two hyenas dogged our steps snickering obscenity. The rest was black, unfathomable night.

But we came at last to a lane that led due northward by the pole-star and Grim led the way up that, following a cart-wheel track beside a wall. And presently we emerged into a clump of pine-trees that were startling because so unexpected in that land, where men have cut for fuel whatever bears no fruit that men can eat and the goats have seen to it that nothing grows again. There were thirty or forty pines with grass beneath them, clean and well-kept.

"Care to see Abraham's Oak?" asked Grim — showman again; he could not rest until you had seen everything. "I think Ali Baba and his gang will come here before dawn; they always used to. We'll have to beat it soon, but you've time to see the tree. There'll be no time afterward."

It stood within two hundred feet of us, surrounded by a stone wall and an iron railing — a veritable oak, so huge and ancient that a man's life seemed an absurd thing as we stood beneath. Under the stars, with shadows all about, it looked vaster than by daylight, its dignity unmarred by signs of decay and only its age and hugeness to be wondered at — those and the silence that it seemed to breathe.

"They had to fence it to keep thieves away," said Grim. "No, not only souvenir-sharps. The thieves of Hebron used to meet under the pines and set their fires against this oak. Abraham is supposed to have pitched his tent under this identical tree, so it must have been big then, and that's three thousand years ago. It has been a rendezvous ever since. Ali Baba loves the spot. Come on."

We passed through a gate and up-hill to where big buildings and a tower loomed lonely against the sky, I too busy wondering about Abraham and that old tree to take any interest in modern convents. The patriarch came from Ur of the Chaldees, wherever that was. What sort of tents did he have, and how many? According to Genesis he must have had a small tribe with him; what did they look like camped around that tree and how were his slaves and retainers armed?

Modern happenings amuse me more when I can follow their roots back into the subsoil of time; but that leads to brown study and hurt shins. I barked mine against a modern American plow, as Grim turned aside along the hilltop and picked up a big stone, to thunder with it on the wooden door of a high square tower.

It stood apart from the convent buildings, modern and unlovely — might have been a belfry, for all you could tell in the dark — perhaps one of those vainglorious beginnings the religious congregations make with thousands of yet-to-be-solicited contributors in mind. The door was opened presently by an old Russian female in a night-cap, who screamed at sight of us.

She knew no Arabic — no English. Grim beckoned the policeman, and his rifle turned out to be a theme she comprehended, for she crossed herself in a quick-fire flurry and stood aside. Grim gave her a coin, for which she blessed him profusely — or so I suppose; the words were Russian — and we entered a square room dimly lighted by a night-light that burned before an ikon in a corner. It formed the whole ground-story of the tower, bedroom and living-room in one, and was chock-a-block with rubbishy furniture, but clean.

In the corner opposite the ikon was an iron stair with a handrail, like one of those that stokers use to emerge by from the boiling bowels of a ship. Grim started up it, but told the policeman to stay below and keep the door shut, presumably to prevent the old lady from communicating with her friends outside — for you never know in Palestine what innocents are earning money on the side by acting as thieves' telegraph. I followed Grim.

Story after story the iron ladder twisted on itself in pitchy blackness, until we came out at last on a flat roof with a waist-high parapet, crossed by two ropes on which the beldame's washing hung — not edifying as a spectacle, nor pleasant when the wind drove it in your face. There was nothing else to see there except the stars that looked almost within reach. Grim leaned his back against the parapet and proceeded to admire them.

"What next?" I asked, for since the only ones I can ever identify are the dipper and the pole-star I soon grow inattentive to astronomy.

"You'd better sleep. Nothing more till sunrise."

So I did. It was pretty chilly up there without a blanket three thousand feet above sea-level, but some of the old lady's damp laundry helped to temper it and the balance went under me to soften contact with the roof. For a few minutes I lay listening to Grim's mellow voice chanting familiar lines, staring upward drowsily and growing almost dizzy with a sense of vastness.

"When I consider thy heavens, the work of thy fingers, the moon and the stars, which thou hast ordained . . ."

But when he changed to Hebrew and boomed out the psalm as it was written by a man who may have wondered at the same sky from the very hill on which we were, I dozed off. Nothing can send you to sleep quicker than a monolog in Hebrew, and I recommend it to the nurse-maids.

When I awoke Grim was still keeping watch, but the stars were paling in the mauve and gold of coming dawn. The policeman had come up. I suppose Grim had been below to fetch him without waking me, and an annoying sense of having been babied by both of them helped dissipate the stiff discomfort and the civilized yearning for a tooth-brush and hot coffee. Besides, I might have missed something.

I came and stood between them where they leaned over the parapet staring downhill past the convent in the direction of the clump of pines and the iron-fenced oak. The great tree developed slowly out of pearl-colored mist as the sun rose, looking weary and decrepit now that the cloak of night was off, its gnarled, gray lower limbs propped up on wooden beams and the huge trunk split under the weight of centuries.

But Grim had seen that tree a hundred times. It needed more than another view of it at dawn to make him and an Arab policeman, born within a mile of it, hang by the waist over that parapet and stare like mast-headed seamen in an Atlantic fog.

"Dahrak! Shuf!" said the policeman suddenly, and both men ducked until their heads were almost level with the masonry. A slight puff of wind rolled the mist apart, producing the effect of turning on more light, and through the iron railings above the wall surrounding the oak I could make out the figures of men squatted in a circle. They might have been gambling, for they faced inward and their heads were close together. Secretive and at least a bit excited they were certainly.

"Now watch 'em!" said Grim. "For God's sake watch 'em!" I think he mistrusted his own eyes after the long vigil.

When the comet-tail of the mist had vanished along the valley in front of a wind that shook down the dew in jeweled showers, the men who sat under the tree rose in a hurry as if they had let time steal a march on them and helped one another over the fence in something of a panic. Then, in single file, they started across country toward the opposite hillside. I counted eighteen of them and the man who led was some one I had never seen before — a man who walked with a limp and wore a *tarboosh* wrapped in calico. The others were unmistakable even at that distance — old Ali Baba and his sons.

"If we lose sight of them we're done for! Tell you what," said Grim, "you and the policeman stay up here. I'll follow them. We ought to manage it between us that way. If it seems to you I'm off the trail, give one long shout; they'll think it's a herdsman rounding up stray cattle, I'll understand and cast again, or wait for you. If you see I'm surely on their heels, you two follow and catch up as fast as you can."

H E REPEATED the instructions to the policeman in Arabic and vanished. While we watched him run down-hill the old woman came up panting, to abuse me in voluble Russian about her crumpled cotton underclothes; but Russian is one of several things I don't know, so we didn't grow intimate. The policeman bundled all her laundry up and threw if off the roof, which seemed to me hardly tactful in the circumstances; so I gave her a coin and she blessed me and we let it go at that.

Thereafter I could hardly watch Grim and the swiftly retreating eighteen for wondering at the view. You could see clear across the whole of Palestine — the Moab Hills beyond the Dead Sea to the eastward, and over to the west the blue of the Mediterranean and thirty miles of white surf pounding on golden sand. A little, little country, that had managed to make more impression on the world than many a big one!

Grim followed as far as the road we had come by in the night without troubling to conceal himself. After that, though, he took to hiding behind rocks and running forward in spurts when he dared. But all that trouble turned out to be unnecessary, for before long we saw all eighteen men disappear behind a scrawny olive-tree in such extraordinary fashion that a cave at that spot was the only possible explanation. It was two thirds of the way up the opposite hill, about a mile, or something less, from where we watched.

So the policeman shooed me off the roof as if I were a goat out of bounds — grumbled at me for taking so much time on the ladder and at the old dame downstairs for not having breakfast ready for us — and panted behind me down the hill with a running comment on the weight of his rifle and the absurdity of racing when a sensible man might walk. He was a perfectly good policeman, raised in the don't-do-it school, and faithful as an old work-horse, with a horse's sense of what is due him on the grades.

We found Grim waiting for us behind a big rock, and when the Arab had recovered breath enough to swear with we got orders to engage.

"Can you see the back of a man's head just beyond the olive-tree? No, not that; that's a hawk feeding; look ten feet to the left. There. See him move? Mahommed ben Hamza keeping lookout. Never occurred to the fool to look this way, or he'd have seen you two experts maneuvering! Now there's just a chance they'll prove ugly. One of us may go West this trip. Spread, and come on them from three sides; then if they cut up rough there'll be at least one of us to break back with the news. I'll snoop up this side and approach first. You two get over the brow of the hill and watch what happens to me. Re-enforce me as required or when I beckon."

So we made a short circuit and ran and lay a hundred yards apart on top of the hill. The policeman raised his rifle and as soon as Grim caught sight of it he left cover and walked straight forward, singing a shepherd song. But quite as clearly as Grim's voice I could hear the drumming of an airplane flying low from the direction of Ludd; and the man outside the cave was watching that intently, so that he neither saw nor heard Grim until he was close up.

The plane circled twice over Hebron and departed. Grim went closer and spoke. I couldn't hear what he said, but Mahommed at the cave-mouth jumped and then put his hands up. Grim ordered him down into the cave and beckoned to us. I did not know until then that Grim had as much as a pistol with him.

The cave was the usual thing. All that country is full of caves and every one of them has been a sepulcher until another generation or any army came and robbed it. There was a low, hewn entrance that you had to stoop to get by, and a short dark passage with a sharp turn, beyond which you could imagine anything you liked. You could enter at your peril; a man couldn't possibly defend himself in the gut where the passage turned.

"They know now who's here," said Grim. "I'm going to take a chance. They've had time to make their minds up. You'd better stay outside."

But I had not had that run on an empty stomach just to cool my heels outside a cave and told him so.

"All right," he laughed. "Suit yourself. We'll leave Mustapha."

But the policeman wouldn't hear of it either and got point-blank mutinous. He asked what sort of figure he would cut going back to the Governorate to report that we had had our throats cut while he looked on. He said he did not mind getting killed, since that was likely to happen just now at any time, and demanded to go in first. So Grim let him fix his bayonet and follow me, with strict orders not to start anything unless we were attacked first.

And after all that fuss there was not any opposition, although there well might have been. Twenty feet beyond the turn the passage opened into an egg-shaped cave, where all eighteen men sat solemnly around a lighted candle. The eighteenth — he of the tarboosh wrapped in calico — looked like a lunatic. They had taken his long knife away — old Ali Baba had it laid across his knees — and two of the sons — the giant and the fellow with the long arms — were sitting one on either side of him, leaning inwards, with the obvious purpose of seizing him if he tried to move.

I HAVE never seen a more ferocious-looking devil. He had a lean, mean face with scars on it and loose lips like an animal's that seemed to have been given him for the purpose of hurling incentive language at a crowd; they made a sort of trumpet when he thrust them out. He had a cataract in one eye, but the other made up for it by being preternaturally bright and black and cunning; and his ears were set far back like an angry dog's.

"Peace! Peace!" urged Ali Baba, as Grim and Mustapha and I stood upright with our backs to the entrance. Grim had put his pistol out of sight, but the policeman stood on guard like a terrier watching rats.

"Peace! Peace!" all sixteen sons repeated after the patriarch.

"Fools! Idiots!" yelled the eighteenth man and tried to spring to his feet, but the men on either side restrained him. I think even a gorilla would have been helpless in those titanic arms that pressed him downward like a cork into a bottle until he seemed a full foot shorter than he actually was and gasped under the strain.

"What will you, Jimgrim?" asked Ali Baba.

Grim nodded in the direction of the eighteenth man.

"I've come for him."

But the gentleman did not propose to be fetched, and he had a way of his own of making the objection obvious. He couldn't move, for the giant on one side and the monstrous-armed fellow on the other continued to lean their weight on him; but he could speak and yell blasphemy and threaten; and he surely did, filling the cave with a clamor like a dog-fight.

The blasphemy was his great mistake, for they were simply a pious gang of thieves, despite their own sacrilege, and his coarsely mouthed Egyptian liberties with sacred words hurt their feelings. They might have taken his part with more determination but for that.

"You fools! Kill them! Kill all three of them!" he yelled and followed it with frightful imprecations — foul, filthy epithets all mixed up with the names of angels and Allah so that Ali Baba protested and his sixteen sons clucked after him in chorus like a lot of scandalized hens.

"What else have you got in the cave besides that beauty?" Grim inquired.

"Nothing, Jimgrim. This is but a meeting-place," said Ali Baba.

"Um-m-m! Nothing under that stone you're sitting on?"

"Nothing, Jimgrim. I am old. The floor of the cave is cold. My sons give me the place of honor."

"Suppose you let me look."

Ali Baba hesitated and collected eyes like a hostess breaking up a dinner-party. It was perfectly obvious that at a word from their chief the whole gang would resist, but Grim stepped into the midst of the circle very coolly with his back to the most dangerous men and waited smiling. I knew what he had in mind. At the first symptom of attack he was going to put his foot on the candle. I got ready to bolt into the throat of the cave ahead of him where, with one rifle and one pistol he and I could keep the lot of them at bay while the policeman could run for help. He told me afterwards that he would have sent me running and kept the policeman by him; so the imaginary glory of a scrap that never happened is not mine after all.

What saved the situation was the Egyptian's tactics. Fired by his own savage imagination he supposed Grim was going to lay hands on Ali Baba and he was one of the all-too-plentiful gentry who believe that numbers are the only unanswerable argument.

"Idiots! Kill him!" he screamed and began to struggle with the men who held him, burying his yellow teeth in the giant's hand and striking out like a great ape simultaneously with arms and legs.

Now that giant was a great good-natured fellow — the apple of old Ali Baba's eye and the pride of the gang. The blood squirted from his hand and the patriarch sprang up from his place to interfere, but not so quickly as the youngest, Mahommed, he who had helped us once at El-Kerak. He sprang across the floor from behind Grim and beat the Egyptian over the eyes with a fist like an olive-knot until he let go, stunned.

Then, while they crowded to make a fuss about the big man's injury Grim very calmly lifted up the stone on which Ali Baba had been sitting. Funnily enough, I expected to see jewels and all the rest of the trimmings of the legendary robbers' cave — golden money at any rate and perhaps a big iron chest with rings to lift it by. But Grim looked perfectly contented with the little paper packages that lay in the hole, neatly fastened with red string and laid in a circle like a clutch of flattened eggs.

"Who stole these from the doctor?" he asked, stowing them carefully away about his person. "You, Ali Baba?"

"Allah forbid! I would not rob the *hakim*. This dog of an Egyptian was in the hospital to have his eyes healed. He knows English and can read the names on labels."

"Did you put him up to it?"

"Not I! He begged a meal from us afterwards and offered to show us how he fooled foreigners for money in the hotels of Massa [Egypt]. So we came with him to this cave, where he had hidden what he stole; and here he breathed fire, and showed us how to do it. But he kept the secret to himself of how to mix the powders, putting the stuff on our tongues and teaching us until we could do it perfectly."

"So you can't work the fire-gift without him, eh?"

"More is the pity!"

"That settles that, then! Did you tell the people what I said about postponing action until tonight?"

"I and my sons. We all spoke of it. Some were angry with us. Some were pleased. Some doubted. But we, who had the fire-gift, had the last word. Jimgrim, we have kept faith."

I went over and looked at the Egyptian, who was still stunned, gurgling through his gruesome mouth and bleeding pretty freely from Mahommed's blows that would have felled a lion. The scars on his face looked like burns at close quarters; and that was likely, for they say that nearly all beginners at that trickster's trade have ghastly accidents.

"What is this about the fire-gift going back, Jimgrim?" Ali Baba asked.

"It goes back tonight."

"And we? Do you mean to put us to shame? Are we to have no hand in this? Is our honor not in your keeping?"

The gang crowded close on Grim to hear his answer, and Mustapha clucked nervously between his teeth, rattling the rifle to call attention to it.

I was as scared as he was, but if Grim minded in the least he did not show it.

"What's this talk about honor?" he asked. "Are you trying to add to the terms of a bargain after it is made?"

"No, no, no!" they chorused and he laughed at them.

"What then?"

"We are your friends," said Ali Baba. *"Inshallah,* a man such as you is thoughtful for his friends!"

"Your friends, Jimgrim, don't forget it!"

"Think of El-Kerak, Jimgrim!"

"Who provided camels for you when you went in pursuit of the Beersheba thieves?"

"When you were governor here, who brought word about the man from Bethesda — he who sought to knife you in the night? Remember that, Jimgrim!"

"Yes, and who slew the fakir who had gone mad?"

"Didn't we save the life of the British officer, who had offended everybody and was mobbed?"

"Yes, and lied afterwards to save him from his own people! We have done everything that you ever asked of us, Jimgrim; isn't our father Ali Baba's honor in your keeping?"

"Well, what is it you want?" asked Grim.

"That we shall not be made the laughing-stock of El-Kalil!" Ali Baba answered solemnly. And at that they all sat down, in a circle as before, with Grim standing in the midst. So he moved the stone deliberately with his foot and sat down too, whereat they all clothed themselves in a new contentment. The Arab thinks far more highly of a judgment given sitting.

"This is a new bargain," Grim began after a moment's thought.

"Inshallah!"

"The terms are these: The old bargain continues until the end of this affair."

"Na'am, na'am. [Yes, yes.]"

"Ali Baba shall retain such personal dignity as I can contrive for him, but the method must be mine."

"Na'am, na'am."

"In return for it, Ali Baba and all his sixteen sons and grand-sons shall be the friends of the present governor, de Crespigny, and of his assistant Jones."

"Taib! They are worthy of it. They are bold. The right spirit is in both of them! We agree!"

"And nothing in this agreement shall be construed to mean that Ali Baba and his gang shall not all or severally go to jail, if convicted of breaking the law in future. They go to jail in the proper spirit, without malice, if caught and convicted."

"Taib! Agreed!"

"Very well," said Grim. "Now three or four of you pick up that Egyptian, and take him to the jail at once!"

CHAPTER VIII

SO WE, who had gone forth that night but a party of three, returned a twenty-man platoon, dumping our prisoner at the jail en route. They lugged him like a corpse with heels trailing, and he hardly recovered consciousness before being locked up, which was a good thing for him as well as us, for he began acting like a caged wild animal at once, yelling as he wrenched at the cell bars, setting both feet against them, cracking huge shoulder-muscles in the effort to break loose.

There was almost a mutiny when Grim insisted on six of Ali Baba's gang offering themselves at once to Dr. Cameron for a body-guard.

"Ask him to come soon, and you hold that Egyptian while he attends to him."

"But Jimgrim, why? Surely such a man is better dead! And he is cunning. Later, when the rage has left him he will make plans and talk to the other prisoners through the bars."

Grim laughed. "And give away the secret of the fire-gift, eh? Tell 'em you haven't it any longer? Too bad!"

"One might go in there and kill him, as if it were by accident," suggested Mahommed ben Hamza genially — he who had done the damage in the first place. "Or I could strike him through the bars, thus!"

"You for the gallows if you dare!" Grim answered. "There's a row of old cells below-ground. Some of you men go down and clean out one of them thoroughly. I'll have him put down there after the doctor's through with him; then, if all's well and you all play the game straight, he shall be taken to Jerusalem."

All except six of them and Ali Baba trooped down-stairs with the easy familiarity of old frequenters of the place. They knew where the brooms and buckets were — whom to ask for soap — where to draw water; the whole routine of that establishment was at their fingers' ends.

But Ali Baba and the six who went to offer their strong service to the doctor had to cool their heels. He was at the Governorate to breakfast, and had brought the nurse with him — a big, raw-boned Scots virgin from the Isle of Lewis in the Outer Hebrides, where they call fish "fush" and the girl who can not do the work of two southron men is not thought much of. I think she could have licked that Egyptian single-handed. She and Cohen were already in an argument about religion, and just as we came in she was telling him he would better mend his doctrine while there was time.

"For Hell's an awful place!"

"Maybe you know?" he suggested. "Tell me some more, miss."

She talked to him about fire and brimstone all through breakfast without any kind of malice but a perfectly sincere desire to scare him into Christianity.

"Ain't you afraid you'll get killed before night?" he asked, trying at last to turn the subject.

But she was not afraid of anything except bad doctrine, and only of that in case it should get by her unrebuked. As Cameron had said the day before, she was a good lass; she would stand.

"Tell me about Heaven," sighed Cohen. "I'm tired of hearin' about Hell."

"Man, man! You may be in Hell before bedtime!" she answered and Grim laughed aloud.

"She's quite right, Aaron. Initiation takes place directly after breakfast. Third degree follows, and Hell tonight!"

All through breakfast there were interruptions. De Crespigny had to keep leaving the table to interview local notables, who called to complain that the city was growing more turbulent every hour and they could not fairly be held responsible.

Jones swallowed a few mouthfuls and started off alone to look alert and confident in the swarming *suk,* since to appear the reverse of afraid was about the only available resource, though that seemed limitless. And just as breakfast finished there came once more the splutter and bark of a motorcycle down-street.

"Can you beat that?" asked de Crespigny, coming in and handing the dispatch to Grim. They let me look at it; in fact, it was passed around the table afterward, although the envelope was stamped **SECRET** as usual in enormous letters:

```
    Your message of yesterday received. Troops here
are busy. Governors of outlying places are
expected to carry on accordingly. A demonstration
will be made by airplane from Ludd this morning;
the pilot will be expected to report whether all
is quiet or otherwise. In the event of his report-
ing all quiet no action is expected to be taken in
your direction before tomorrow morning, when a
Sikh patrol will be sent with machine guns if it
```

can be spared. Please report by bearer if there
are any symptoms of a concerted attack on Jerusalem, rumors having reached us.

It was signed by the same staff-major who had written the message of the day before. But this time there was a foot-note, not
typewritten but in the angular long-hand of the administrator
himself.

Carry on, boys. Kettle.

"That postscript's typical of 'Pots and Pans'," said Grim. "I'll
bet he's sent help to some of the weak sisters elsewhere and
counts on you fellows to worry through. There's probably a raid
in force coming up from the Jordan Valley and every available
man in Jerusalem combed up to deal with it. How will you
answer?"

De Crespigny wrote two lines and showed them:

*Carrying on, sir. No sign of attack on Jerusalem from this place
yet. Sikhs welcome when available.*

"Good!" said Grim. "He likes telegrams. Man fired at on the
way?"

"Says not."

"That proves nothing," put in Cameron. "I've been five-and-
twenty years here, and know their ways. They're flocking into
the city. So the fields are deserted. The Turks understood how to
deal with them. The Turks, in a crisis like this, would have
hanged out of hand any man found in the streets who did not
belong to the city. I've seen them strung up in front of the jail in a
row like haddock drying in the sun. Djemal Pasha would have
straightened out this business in less than half a day. He was a
rascal, though; he'd have lined his pockets afterwards with fines
that would have kept them all too poor to make trouble for a year
to come! Well, we're not Turks and they're gone. But I heard ex-
president Roosevelt speak in Egypt. 'Rule or get out!' That was
his advice. Speaking as a missionary, I'd say take the latter half
of it — get out! Teach, yes, if they'll listen; but teach 'em what?
They're as moral as we are. Teach 'em our Western commercial-
ism? God forbid! Literature? We don't read our own books, so
why should they? Which of you can quote me half a line from
Robbie Burns?"

"Speaking of burns, Doc," put in Grim, "You've got to teach me some chemistry before lunch — something to prevent them."

"I'm a very busy man."

"Have you plenty of drugs?"

"I've plenty of nothing! Fifteen hundred pounds a year our Mission scrapes together for this hospital, and out of that must come my salary, if, as and when I choose to draw it. I've drawn it seven times in twenty years. Ye'd think Hebron would contribute something; it did at times under the Turks; but now all the rascals do is steal my stores. Teach, eh? Come wi' me to the hospital and I'll show ye how one man and one trained nurse care for eighty patients in a forenoon."

So COHEN, Grim and I walked over with him and the lady from the Hebrides and he barked with pleasure at sight of the paper packets that Grim laid on his office table in the trim stone mission building.

"This man Cohen has got to be made fire-proof!" Grim announced.

Cameron smiled.

"Has Miss Gordon's sermon made him so afraid of Hell as that?"

"The point is, can you do it for us, Doc? Or must we experiment?"

"Well, there are preparations that so indurate the cuticle as to render it insensible to a very high degree of heat."

"Are the ingredients in these packets?"

"Aye, some of them. These could be improved on."

"What would you add?"

"Quicksilver, but I've none to spare. I think I can recall a formula, though, that I once used for the hands of a Turkish soldier who was employed in the castle armory on some hot metal work. Let's see — mnmn — spirit of sulfur — onion juice — essence of rosemary — *sal ammoniac*— that's all. You could make a paste of these drugs on the table, but it would be liable to form a hard film that might crack, with dangerous consequences. The other's better; I've a notion it's what they used in mediaeval times when people went through the ordeal by fire — walking on hot plowshares, ye know, and all that hocus-pocus."

"Here's your patient," said Grim. "Make him Hell-proof, please!"

He pulled Cohen forward by the arm and the poor chap's face changed color under the tan.

"Why me? Say, I'm not afraid of Hell! You quit your kiddin'! I've had about enough of this practical jokin'! That tank in the dark was my positively last performance!"

"Listen, old man — we've nobody but you," said Grim. "You've got to carry the big end. All we can do is support you and watch points. You know perfectly well it would be no use trying to argue with the Jews of this place; we've got to show them. If you prove to them you can handle fire without getting burned and I prove to them that they'll all be dead before night unless they sit into the game, we can make at least some of them play. It's the only chance. If you should back down now, we're done for! Go ahead, Doc — mix the devil's undershirt. See that Satan has nothing on this man when it comes to squatting on the slag!"

"What? Have I got to sit on fire? Without pants?"

"No, not as bad as that."

"There's a word of advice I'll give ye," said Cameron. "It's a simple matter to treat a man's skin so that he can sit on hot coals, or walk on them, or take them in his hands. Ye may even put them in your mouth; but there's the danger. That's very dangerous. Ye can treat the inside of a man's mouth so that flame won't hurt it; but ye can't reach the membrane of the throat or the lungs and I wouldn't change places with the man who breathed flame inward!

"That's how most of these fire-eaters ye see performing in Cairo and places like that come to a bad end. They don't die so quickly but they've time to suffer the agony of the damned. I'd recommend ye to be very careful. And mind ye, I'm not asking what ye're up to. It's none o' my business."

It was a long job squeezing out the juice of onions and mixing up the different ingredients, but Grim and I lent a hand and Cohen watched like a victim getting ready for the stake. He had a feeling, that nobody could blame him for, of being put upon; and his naturally alert business instinct made him suspicious of taking what looked like more than his share of the risk, to say nothing of the physical danger involved in fooling with fire.

But Grim kept talking to him and did not make the mistake of minimizing what he had to do. He took the other line, making use of rather subtle flattery, saying how lucky we were to have a genuine, sure-fire American Jew to show the Orthodox crowd of Hebron how to save themselves.

But there wasn't really the least doubt about Cohen. He would kick and complain for the simple business purpose of emphasizing his stake in the proceedings; that much was second nature. And he was certainly afraid; but so was I, and I don't think Grim felt any too confident under his mask of cool amusement. But if Grim had told Cohen he was slated for sure death, though he would have argued the point undoubtedly, I'm pretty sure he would have gone ahead.

As a matter of fact, none of us was fooling himself very seriously about the chance of surviving that night's work. The prospect was too slim altogether. There were too many opportunities for a slip, however carefully and cunningly Grim might stage-manage the affair. Besides, we had not yet converted the Orthodox Jews of Hebron to our plan; and to lift up a mountain by the roots and plant it in the sea might prove not much more difficult than to persuade those frozen-souled conservatives.

It was best not to try to imagine what might happen if we were detected playing tricks with Moslem prejudices — as might easily turn out. The Sheikh of the mosque, for instance, might turn cold at the last minute and denounce us as the best way out of his own predicament.

But Cohen was finally stripped to the waist to an accompaniment of joshing, and every inch of his skin was covered carefully with the preparation. Then that was allowed to dry and the whole performance was repeated, until at last Cameron pronounced him fire-proof from the waist upwards. But he doubted it volubly, until Grim struck a match and made the first test, holding the flame against his body in a dozen places without producing the least sensation.

After that it was vaudeville. Cohen's spirits rose and his imagination with them. He staged a whole performance, and ballyhooed it in the bargain like a small-town circus side-show performer.

"Ladies and gents, you mayn't believe it, but the guy who ought to spill the talk for me is sick. After my performance at the last town I was red-hot and he feared I'd set the bed on fire. So he took a bucket of water and threw it over me. The water turned to steam and scalded him. Now watch! The original and only noncombustible asbestos man!"

Cameron had to hurry through his hospital and then go to the jail to attend to the Egyptian, held down by the iron hands of Ali Baba's men. So he lent Grim a battered old book on ancient magic and left us.

Cohen was so full of high spirits and original ideas for stunts by that time that it was quite a job to get him to pay attention, but Grim took as much pains with him as if he were a performing animal. Ali Baba had to be brought in, anointed with the dope and taught too, for the old Arab's accomplishment was crude and limited, although he was a first-class showman in his own way.

Thereafter the whole plan for the night's unlawful ritual had to be worked out in detail and there Ali Baba was a great help, for he understood the Arab mind and knowing Hebron of old could judge to a nicety just what would produce an effect and what would not. The hardest thing was to get Cohen imbued with a proper sense of solemnity, for he had a perfectly entire disrespect for every kind of ritual and was constitutionally inclined to make low comedy of it.

Again and again Grim impressed on him, Ali Baba seconding, the certainty that we, and every Jew in Hebron, would be killed that night unless he kept a straight face. He had no feeling for tribal history; none for pageantry; every suggestion Grim made he capped with a caricature of it.

"Say, when I reach the mosque steps, suppose I throw the fire in the Sheikh's face and set alight to his beard, what then?"

The rehearsal was cut short by the noise of rioting. We were hardly a quarter of a mile from the Governorate and through the open window came the yelling of a mob that surged by the Governorate gate. It bore no resemblance to the singing of the men who had come dancing up-street the previous day, but was shriller voiced, without rhythm, and there was the ominous mob-growl underneath it like the anger of a hundred upset hives.

"Ah!" remarked Ali Baba dryly. "That will be the end of it all! No fire-gift tonight! Better run, Jimgrim! Run for Jerusalem while there is time! I would be sorry to see you with your throat cut!"

Grim was listening and signed to Ali Baba to be still. It was difficult to pick out words from the babel of noise down-street, for the uproar came from a thousand throats; but it was clear they were shouting for de Crespigny, and that was a good sign as far as it went. If they had intended murder they would have rushed the building, instead of calling for the governor to come and talk to them.

Suddenly Grim ran from the room and I after him. I didn't stop to reason it out, but followed intuitively — partly from a sense of dependence on his swift wit and also because it's easier, though not nearly always wiser, to meet trouble half-way than to sit and wait for it.

W E RAN out through a side door into a garden and followed a wall fronting on the road. At the far end was a rambling old barn-like building that nearly faced the Governorate. We entered that by climbing the wall at the end of the garden and in another minute were lying on the roof overlooking the crowd.

"Good Lord!" said Grim. "They've got the Chief Rabbi with them! It's all up to young Crep now!"

To say they "had" the Rabbi was to state it very mildly. They had dragged him by the beard and driven him with blows. They held him now in their midst, bruised and terrified, while thirty or forty young Jews and one pathetically brave policeman strove to force their way through the crowd and rescue him — all yelling at the top of their lungs and being yelled at.

When de Crespigny came to the gate at last he was not smiling. I think that boy could have smiled in the face of torturers, for he had the priceless gift of self-control and an inborn faith in the value of a grin. But, as he said afterward, crowds vary; sometimes it pays to laugh at them, but at others the suggestion of a smile will goad them into fury. The man who smiled at that crowd would probably have paid for the indiscretion with his life.

As he reached the gate they thrust the Rabbi forward to confront him; but if the Jew deduced from that that he was going to get first word in he was wildly wide of the mark. Ten Arabs, holding the old man by the clothing, foaming at the mouth with emphasis and gesticulating like fish-wives, denounced him to the governor all together, while the crowd tossed in reminders and the Jews on the outskirts shrilled rejoinders. You couldn't make head or tail of it, except that they were threatening de Crespigny. And as everybody talked at once he couldn't understand them either.

"Touch and go!" said Grim to me. "Crep's got the wind up! Lord send he keeps his head!"

De Crespigny watched his chance and then picked out the noisiest, most violent man to do the talking — a very wise move that, for it let off steam.

"Now," he demanded, "what is it?"

"This cursed Jew is a thing they call a Rabbi. He is their leader. He should die. He has defied us and says you will protect him. The Sheikh of the Mosque of Er-Rahman had a vision concerning the fire-gift. It was stolen by thieves for use against the Jews, so the Jews are to return it or be slain! We went to this Rabbi to tell him what he must do tonight, and to make arrangements; but the father of lies swore he knew nothing about it and, what is more, would do nothing!"

"Nothing! I know nothing, nothing! What do I know of any fire-gift?" said the Rabbi.

"Perhaps he doesn't!" said de Crespigny.

"He lies! He does! One was released from the jail this morning, who says he knows the thieves no longer have the fire-gift. So the Jews must have it! Who else?"

"Kill the liar! Kill him!" yelled the rear ranks that were close enough to hear.

De Crespigny looked up, for inspiration probably, and caught sight of Grim's face peering over the roof. Grim nodded violently, that being the only available signal for "go ahead." De Crespigny seemed to understand, and smiled at last.

"I know a way to persuade the Jews," he said. "They no doubt have the fire-gift and they shall return it tonight. Leave the Rabbi and his friends here. I'll see justice done!"

"Good boy!" Grim muttered. "That young Crep has gall and guts. Couldn't be better! Now we've got the Rabbi with the wind up where he can't talk back and can't refuse! Oh, good!"

CHAPTER IX

"I am Rabbi, not governor!"

CROWDS in those latitudes gather and disperse as suddenly as storms and, like the storms, leave a change of atmosphere behind them. In a sense they resemble waterspouts, destructive as the very devil if allowed to boil along unchecked — always fooling themselves that they are doing good, and hiding their real motive from themselves under a noisy pretense of moral purpose. And they can be handled in much the same way as a waterspout, with pretty much the same result. If you can sever the nexus, as it were, between the clouds and the sea — remove the connecting link between a mob and its desire — all's calm again; or, if not calm, then at any rate much safer. There are typhoons, too, that have to be ridden out.

The nexus in this instance was the Jews and the underlying motive, loot. Ever since the heel of the Turk had been lifted the Moslems of Hebron had been aching to loot somebody. Turkish governor after governor had wrung from them in fines and taxes every piastre that he could and given nothing at all in return for it. So they were poor; and if the Jews weren't rich, they were supposed to be.

Not even the Hebron crowd that prides itself on thieving will lay plans to loot a whole quarter of the town and cut three thousand throats without establishing a moral issue first to stalk behind. All humans act that way in the mass and if Hebron is not thoroughly human it is nothing. So old Ali Baba and his fire-gift had come, like many another apparent miracle, in the nick of time to salve the public conscience.

I never found out just to what extent Ali Baba had been opportunist. He may have planned the whole thing with a view to looting; but I think not. I think he only boasted of having planned it, after receiving instruction in the cave from that Egyptian devil; for Ali Baba and all his sixteen sons and grandsons were too childish and direct to have thought the thing out in the first instance. It takes Egypt to invent such a dark scheme.

But whoever invented it, Grim saw through it. He knew Hebron too intimately not to be sure that the Jews would be in deadly danger whenever any sort of uprising occurred anywhere in southern Palestine. Given loyal troops enough, any one can suppress a mob; but the trouble had come at a moment when all the troops were occupied elsewhere, so the solution demanded genius. And genius is always simple, although it has a way of seeming subtly baffling to the onlooker.

It would be absurd to pretend that I, or any one but Grim himself, saw until afterward the thin thread of principle he followed to the final solution. But you can see it now. He established a clear issue. Without once showing his own hand, he pinned the Moslems down to a definite claim against the Jews.

All that remained after that was to get the Jews to pay the claim. Even a fanatically angry mob that receives what it demands needs time in which to formulate a new cause; and time meant the arrival of Sikhs and their machine guns.

But the Jews of Hebron are a cagey, self-reliant and suspicious crew. Any one who had survived among Moslems under Turkish rule in that place would have to be. They no more trusted Grim and de Crespigny than Aaron Cohen, whom they despised as a renegade; and to get them to see the point and play Grim's game until troops should come was about as easy as getting Scottish Highlanders to invest in foreign loans.

The crowd dispersed sulkily, shepherded by the lone policeman gamely parading his authority, and leaving the Rabbi and his friends in the Governorate, where they crowded the hall full and noisily abused de Crespigny for having permitted their Chief Rabbi to be outraged. They seemed to think, or pretended to think that the whole affair was his sole fault, and that he could restore order in a minute if he chose to.

We went and fetched Cohen from the hospital and thrust our way through their midst into the sitting-room, where Grim sent for the Rabbi at once. He refused to come in alone, but brought three friends with him, so we made a party of eight, facing one another across the table; and the din in the hall was so prodigious that whoever spoke had to bellow in order to be heard. Have you ever noticed how the need to shout at a man makes for rising temper? There was not much love lost at that session.

The Rabbi began by refusing point-blank to have anything to do with the fire-gift. He consulted his friends in Spanish, which none of us could understand; and they agreed with him. You would have thought we were asking for a loan of money on poor security to see the look of scandalized disapproval on their faces.

Asked by de Crespigny why he should refuse to countenance a plan that had been devised for the safety of himself and his people, the Rabbi answered that he had nothing to do with politics and refused to interfere.

"Suppose we were to refuse to interfere and just let you get massacred?" de Crespigny retorted.

"But that is your business!" said the Rabbi. "You are the governor. You receive a salary to keep the peace. I am Rabbi, not governor!"

"Have you any alternative suggestion?" de Crespigny asked him.

"Give us rifles! We will defend ourselves."

"In the first place," said, de Crespigny, "I haven't them."

The Rabbi looked utterly incredulous.

"There's one each here for the police and the jailer, two or three revolvers and a pistol. That's all. There's hardly any ammunition. What other suggestion can you make?"

Grim was sitting back watching faces. I don't know whether he had a solution in mind or not; it looked like an *impasse*.

The Rabbi turned and talked in Spanish with his friends.

"It is your business," he said at last in Arabic. "We are not able to do anything. If we are attacked, we shall defend ourselves to the last. If you wish to prevent a massacre you should send for Sikhs."

"There's no knowing when the Sikhs can get here," said de Crespigny. "You're asked to help us gain time by pretending to return that fire-gift to the tomb of Abraham. Surely that's not much?"

"Ah! It will be said afterward that we took liberties with the Moslem religion. It will only be a further excuse for a massacre." We must have made a strange picture arguing the point over that table with its near-art cover and the flowers between us crammed into two brass cartridge cases that the Germans had left behind. De Crespigny and Cohen were the only men in modern costume. The Rabbi and his friends were dressed pretty much as the Pharisees were in Bible days, and bearded in keeping with it. Their faces wore the ivory pallor that comes of ghetto life, and were blanched beneath it with fear that has already passed through all the panic stages and is obstinate at last. They were minded to commit themselves to nothing, those men; skeptical of all promises; incredulous of any man's good-will.

De Crespigny began to lose his temper. It is bad enough at twenty-six to have the lives of thousands on your hands, without being regarded as an enemy by the men you are trying to save.

"God damn you, Rabbi! Don't you see that your refusal means a death sentence for us all?"

"Tch-tch! I sentence no one! I am not responsible for this. I will take no part in it!"

De Crespigny glanced at Grim hopelessly.

"I pass, Grim. Can you say anything?"

Grim nodded.

"Cut loose, Cohen. Tell 'em your views."

I don't know whether Cohen took Grim by surprise or not. He surely astonished the rest of us. I've never seen a man handle a meeting with half such passionate wrath. He grew suddenly red in the face as if he could command his rage to order; stood up; threw off his jacket on the floor; rolled up his shirt sleeves, and sat down again. Then he brought his fist down on the table with a crash that upset both vases and, as Grim had suggested that he should, cut loose.

Arabic was the speech he used, with occasional bursts of English when expletives failed him; and he reeled off a list of the faults of the ancient Jewish race with a completeness and fervor that would start a riot if set down in print.

"You old moss-backs!" he fairly yelled at last. "You silly old suckers! You think I care, perhaps, if you all get your throats cut! Guess again! You're dummies, that's what you are! Marionettes! You're goin' to be used! Who's goin' to use you? Me! Yours truly!"

Then back into Arabic again, reeling out abuse until he gasped for breath.

"Gimme a drink, some one! Now, you left-overs, listen to me! You haven't a word to say! You'll do izzactly as you're told! This plan's all thought out, an' you'll fall in with it! That fire goes back tonight — see? I'm the feller that takes it back — I take the risk, too! I'll show you — watch!"

He sprang to his feet again and stripped himself naked to the waist; then seized the lamp on the side-board, jerked out the wick arrangement, poured kerosene into his hand and rubbed it on his stomach. Next he struck a match and set it alight. "There! That's what!" He smothered the fire with his hands again.

"Tonight I go to the Ghetto. Ali Baba breathes on me and I burn like the Fourth o' July. I'm a Jew, and you'll acknowledge me! Two hundred Sephardim will come along behind me in procession to the tomb of Abraham, chantin' hymns, an' doin' it all in first-class style, or I'll take the fire an' throw it in your face, and tell the Moslems to go get it from you! D'you believe me? So help me God, I'll do it!"

"And that would be the end of every living Jew in El-Kalil," said Grim, quietly approving.

"You are a bad man to talk that way!" the Rabbi objected.

"Bad man? Sure, I'm a Hell of a bad man! Throwin' fire in fellers' faces is meat to me! D'ye see this young officer here? He's a decent feller. D'ye see these others? They're friends o' mine — bad men — bad as me — worse! D'ye think I'm goin' to stand by an' see them get their throats cut without makin' sure that you goody-goodies get yours first? Huh! If there's goin' to be a massacre tonight it starts in the Ghetto, an' the Rabbi is goin' to be number one for the knife! So suit yourselves, only make your minds up quick!"

"We shall stay here — here in this place!" the Rabbi announced suddenly.

"Not you! I'm goin' to kick you out into the street five minutes from now!"

"The governor must protect us!"

"Must he? You try him! Here he is listenin' to what I say! I happen to know izzactly what he'll do; soon as I've kicked you out, he'll call for his cops to chase you down to the Ghetto where you belong! No; you've got your last chance; take or leave it! Who's got a watch? Clock 'em, some one. Give 'em three minutes to decide!"

Grim pulled out Cohen's own gold watch that had been the means of introducing him to all the trouble and laid it on the table ostentatiously, face upward.

"Time starts now!" he announced.

Cohen proceeded to put his shirt on, as if he always made a point of doing that before committing acts of violence; he looked something like a gladiator fitting on his mail — a muscled, beefy man, perfectly able to carry out his threat.

The Rabbi looked imploringly at de Crespigny for any sign of weakness, but was met by a smile whose enigmatic corners suggested anything but that. He tried to consult with his friends, but they thrust back the responsibility on him with shrugging shoulders and something vague about making complaint to Jerusalem later on.

"Thirty seconds more!" announced Grim and Cohen started for the door to open it.

"It is a scandal; but you compel me!" said the Rabbi, throwing up both hands, palms upward.

"Compel nothing!" Cohen retorted hotly. "You choose!"

"I have no choice. I am in the hands of determined men; what can I do?"

"Do you agree to the proposal?" asked de Crespigny. "I must!"

"No side-stepping!" said Grim. "We want a definite affirmative. Will you or won't you?"

"Very well, I will. But there should be a writing — something in writing to prove afterwards that I am not responsible. This is none of my doing. I must not interfere with Moslem prejudices. I can not accept the blame for it. You must absolve me." Grim's eyes met de Crespigny's curiously across the table.

"How about it, Crep? If the old bird wants to be nasty afterward they may have to make an official goat of some one."

"Oh, what's the odds? I'll sign it."

"Don't you!" broke in Cohen. "I'm the guy that forced him. Let me sign it! No reason why you should lose your job for this. The worst they can do to me is fire me out of the country. Come on, write him out a paper and I'll sign it."

"You're a good scout, Aaron," Grim answered, "but we won't let you do it all. Rabbi, you write your own acquittal and I'll put my name on it. I'm responsible for this."

CHAPTER X

"We must score the last trick with the deuce of spades!"

COHEN took charge of the training of the Rabbi and his men; not that they would not have preferred almost any one else, for their scorn of him was marrow-deep. He had a certain amount of kindly feeling for them; they none for him whatever. Those timid old last-ditch conservatives had clung to their orthodoxy in the face of worse calamity than Cohen had ever dreamed of; and the pride that accompanies all conservatism had fossilized their humanity to a point where almost nothing mattered except form and ritual.

Most of them traced descent to ancestors who had been driven from Spain by Ferdinand and Isabella and so added to a natural pride of race and creed an unnatural, exotic arrogance copied from the Dons.

But Cohen was for that very reason exactly the man to handle them. He had just enough sympathy to understand them and know what verbal shafts would surest sting them into obedience. He knew enough to threaten — too much to strike; to mock their pride and yet play up to it. And his business brain was working; he had grasped the extent of the possibilities and was keener now on making the most of the situation than on saving his own skin and ours.

I suspect that at the back of that bull-necked head of his he already had a scheme for making money out of the adventure somehow; if so, I am equally sure he abandoned it afterward, because, although a man of his parts might build up a business with the Hebron *suk,* the same amount of energy and intrigue expended elsewhere would bring at least ten-fold return. But he went at the training of those "Orthodoxies," as he called them, with the zeal of a man who sees money at the other end.

That left Grim free for equally important things and he took them in proper order.

"Crep," he said, "will you be a good fellow and go to the Mosque — don't send, go yourself — and bring the Sheikh here. I'm going to curl up and sleep until he comes."

"All right. In a hurry to see him?"

"No. My guess is that the more parading about the city you do the better. You and Jonesy and the Sheikh might do worse than interview the notables. Get the crowd so keen on tonight's show that they'll have no time to think of much else. Time's the main thing, remember. We must gain time. Every minute of delay brings the arrival of the Sikhs a minute nearer. Better time the affair for ten o'clock. That may mean that some of 'em'll be too sleepy afterward to care for anything but bed. Dawn may see the Sikhs on the road. Bring the Sheikh here when you're good and ready — any time before dark will do. But for the love of Mike, Crep, don't tell him who I am — yet!"

"Your name means something in this place."

"Maybe. But if he learns in advance that I've been in his mosque in disguise with a Jew and another American he'll get rabies! Afterward it won't matter; we'll have the goods on him afterward! You keep up the fake about my being a messenger from Seyyid Omar of El-Kudz, or we'll have the whole nest of wasps about our ears yet!"

So de Crespigny rode horseback into the city, acting on the well-established principle that however clumsy and inconvenient the horse might be in narrow streets, the man on his back looks like personified authority and commands more respect from the crowd than a man on foot.

That is particularly true in the case of Arabs, who think more of a man on a horse than in a motor-car. No mechanical appliance less than a machine gun makes much impression on their minds; the gun means power; the horse means dignity; most other modern trappings either excite cupidity or else contempt.

Grim curled up like a dog and slept on the window-seat as soon as de Crespigny had gone — unconscious almost the moment that he closed his eyes. That trick of sleeping like an animal whenever you so choose is only a forgotten gift; most men can pick it up again, like the sense of smell, that belongs to men as much as to the beasts and is far more valuable, really, than sight or hearing.

A deaf and blind man can still smell his way along, and know more of his surroundings than the ordinary man with eyes and ears intact, who hardly uses them. And as for that trick of sleep, it makes you independent of the clock and furlongs in the race ahead of others, who have to go to bed at stated intervals. It is one of the great good things that living in towns has stolen from us.

But Grim was not destined to sleep long. At the end of about an hour Jones came in looking worried and sat down to write a letter to his girl in England. That was hardly a good symptom. Grim came out of his sleep one eye at a time, the way a dog does exactly, without apparent cause, and lay still for about two minutes watching Jones's back.

"What's wrong, Jonesy?" he asked suddenly.

"Oh, you awake? We've a chance left — one! You couldn't get much for it!"

"What's happened?"

"News from Jerusalem. A couple of men got through on foot with word that the Moslems there have been pretty thoroughly suppressed. They say the administrator has taken the part of the Jews and the Jews are crowing about it. So the Moslems cornered Crep in the city and demanded permission to march on Jerusalem and help their co-religionists. He refused, of course; and they don't want to miss tonight's show — they'll wait for that. We'd better spin it out, because as soon as it's over they're going to put us out of business and cut loose!"

"But hasn't Crep got a pledge from the head-men?"

"Sure. They'll stand by that. They say that if the Jews of this place bring back the fire-gift tonight as promised they'll spare them. But they haven't made any promise to spare us and they're going to blot out the Jerusalem Jews whether we like it or not. They won't believe there are no rifles in the Governorate, so they're coming here first — soon as the show's over!"

"What's Crep doing now?"

"Arresting a few of the noisiest ones. I brought along half a dozen and left them in the jail. I'm going back there now to stand by and stiffen the jail guard. So long, in case my number's up!"

He went out again, examining his revolver and Grim got off the window-seat to pace the floor a time or two.

"Maybe I'd better send you," he said. "It's thirty miles. D'you think you could reach Jerusalem on foot by midnight?"

"What's the matter with a camel?"

"You'd be held up. You're all right until the camel hits a good sharp clip; after that they'd spot you for a white man from a mile away. You'll have to walk in that disguise, and take your chance with the sentries outside Jerusalem."

"Ask for Sikhs, I suppose?"

"Yes. Sorry to have to do it. 'Fraid we must. I'd hoped to help these boys pull through without squealing. Do 'em both good with the Administration. Having to yell for help means they'll get no credit for all that's gone before. Damnit! I hate to do it."

So did I hate it. Setting aside the mere physical exertion of the thirty-mile run, with a good chance of getting knifed or potted on the way and an even better one of being "spiked" by a British sentry in the dark under Jerusalem's walls, I did not want to miss the big event.

"If I get mine on the road," I objected, "you'll be no better off than you were before."

"No. But you'll have done your best along with the rest of us."

You couldn't answer that. I pulled my boots off, to put soap on my socks.

"Better give me some grub in a handkerchief and lend me a gun, then."

"Sure."

But he did nothing about it. He was pacing the floor again, thinking.

"No!" he said suddenly. "Two of Ali Baba's men must make the trip. If one gets scuppered, the other may get through. I'll give them two identical letters. They'll hate to do it, but I can talk the old man round and they'll obey him. But it's rotten having to squeal after all this! Damn! I hate it! Jiminy! No! Wait! By gorry, man; I'll be durned if I won't try that first!"

"Try what?"

But one of a dozen things you can never make Grim do is talk over the details of a plan that is only half-formed in his mind. He quit pacing the floor, and went and squatted Arab-fashion on the window-seat again.

I DID not get a glimmer of what he intended until half an hour later de Crespigny came in, bringing the Sheikh of the mosque with him. Grim gave the Sheikh the window-seat and took the darker corner for himself; taking the hint, I squatted in the curtained alcove leading to the hall, where I might be presumed to be door-keeper and could overhear without being too much seen.

Grim began by asking the Sheikh what arrangements he had made for the night and listened gravely, making no comment.

"Do you think the whole plan is good?" he asked at last.

"Allah! It is your plan! How should you ask that?"

"I propose to call it off!" said Grim and even de Crespigny gasped.

"*Ma bisir abadan!* [That will never do!] Call it off now, after I have stood up in the mosque before all the people and told of a vision and persuaded them and all? How can you call it off? They will simply massacre the Jews!"

"No. It seems to me it would be simpler after all to tell the truth about it."

"Who will believe you?"

"Every one! I have the man who invented the whole trick as well as those who carried it out. They are all Moslems. I propose to tell the people quite simply that the whole thing was a trick, with you a party to it. I can go and talk to them when they gather before the mosque tonight. They might kill the Jews then, afterward, but attend to you first!"

"And you! They would kill you too!"

"Perhaps. But why me? I don't think that in the circumstances they would kill a British officer, who had exposed you for playing tricks on them!"

"A British officer? I don't understand."

"I'm a British officer."

"You?"

"Sure. Used to be Governor of Hebron. Grim's my name. I'm better known as Jimgrim."

"Hah! Then that is simple! Denounce me tonight. *Taib!* I will denounce you for having entered the mosque by a trick. I will denounce you for sacrilege!"

"All right. Then they'll kill us both."

"But what good will that do you, Jimgrim?"

"No good."

"Nor me either!" The Sheikh laughed like a man who believes he is conversing with a lunatic.

"If you don't want to be exposed tonight," said Grim, "you'd better offer to make terms."

"Terms about what?"

"You know as well as I do that the mob is planning to attack this Governorate after tonight's ceremony, kill everybody in it, plunder it of arms, and march on Jerusalem."

"I can do nothing about that."

"Yes you can."

"Allah!"

"You can think up some way of keeping the crowd idle until morning."

"I? They will not listen to me outside the mosque."

"All right. Talk to 'em inside the mosque."

"I have talked enough. I have already accepted risk enough. My place is enough in danger as it is."

"Can't you have another vision?"

"*Mustahil!* [Impossible!] They have had enough of visions! They are simple people, but determined. They intend to march on Jerusalem to protect their co-religionists before it is too late. Who can stop them?"

"You can. You can hold them until it's too late to make the attempt."

"I? How?"

"You know as well as I do what will happen to them. They'll be met by machine guns outside the walls of Jerusalem and mowed down."

"I can not help that!"

"Yes you can. It's up to you. If that happens it will be on your head! Now, if we're willing to go through with this performance tonight to save your position for you at the mosque, you ought to be willing to go a step further to save that crowd from the machine guns. Never mind about us. Consider the crowd."

"*Ya hain!* [Oh, the pity of it!] How I regret that I did not denounce those thieves in the first place!"

"Regret's no good! What are you going to do now; that's the point. See here: If you'll — yes, that'll do the trick! — most of the ringleaders will be inside the mosque, for they're a holy lot of rascals! — if you'll get up in the pulpit and give them a long harangue to the effect that your spirit tells you to warn them — to go slow — to be cautious — to wait for the word; and that you'll give 'em the word at the proper minute — you can leave the rest to us; and we'll fix it so that you get credit as a prophet. Will you do that?"

"*Taib.* I will do it. But I doubt that it will do any good."

"All right, that's a bargain, then." Grim turned to the governor. "Crep, old boy, trumps are all out; we must score the last trick with the deuce of spades!"

CHAPTER XI

"Allahu akbar! La illahah il-allah!"

YOU know that feeling at a melodrama of the old sort, when all the villain's plans are prospering and a ghastly death stares the hero in the face; even although some fool has told you the plot in advance, so that you know what the end is going to be, you can't pretend not to be all worked up about it. And most men — and more women — have faced at some time the imminent risk of death, with just one chance of pulling through.

Well, we enjoyed both sensations that night. We were spectators of a play and actors in it, not knowing yet whether it was comedy or tragedy. We hoped we could foresee the end, but weren't at all sure.

"We're betting on the merest guess," said Grim. "We may as well not fool ourselves. Perhaps we can hold the crowd until tomorrow morning. Perhaps not. If we succeed, perhaps the Sikhs will come. We're betting they'll come. If they do, good; Crep and Jonesy'll be slated for promotion. If they don't, we'll none of us need rations ever any more, amen! Let's go."

It was about nine o'clock — no moon — and the roar of El-Kalil was like the voice of a long tunnel full of railway trains, made all the more unholy by utter darkness. After a long consultation de Crespigny had left two policemen on guard at the jail and taken the other eight with him.

The lonely little one-horse plan finally decided on, as the best possible in the event of an outbreak, was for de Crespigny and his eight police to fight their way to the jail, gather up the two guards, the jailer and his assistant, leave the jail and prisoners to the mob, and fall back on the Governorate. The rest of us were to join de Crespigny if we could and Doctor Cameron and the nurse were to take their chance of being unmolested at the hospital, seeing that neither of them would hear of any other course.

It was decided that to make a last stand at the hospital, supposing we could ever reach it, would only seal the fate of two people whom the mob might otherwise treat as noncombatants.

De Crespigny had ridden off, with his eight policemen tramping stolidly behind him, awfully afraid, yet proud as Lucifer to be the bodyguard of Law where no law would be otherwise, and encouraged by the sight of his brave young back bolt-upright in the saddle. A man's back often tells a truer story than his face.

Grim and I went on foot — to the Ghetto first, leaving Jones alone in the Governorate; for somebody had to hold headquarters, and the joyless job is the junior's by right of precedent. Grim had a word to say to the jail-guards on the way and we reached without incident the narrowing gut where the street passes into the city by a fragment of the ancient wall.

From that point onward it was one long struggle to force a way through the crowd. All Hebron was out, trying to win to the Ghetto gate and see the preliminaries. There was not room in the street for seven men to stand abreast, nor space by the Ghetto for a crowd of fifty; yet several thousand men were milling and crushing for a front view, like long-horn steers that smell water — and all in the dark. You couldn't see the face of a man three paces off.

We soon got jammed up hopelessly and only contrived to keep together by clinging and wrestling. The hilt of a man's sword took me under the ribs and pressed until I nearly yelled aloud with agony. I trod on his instep to give him a different sense of direction and if he could have drawn the sword I should have learned the feel of its sharper end. He started an argument, spitting out the savage abuse within six inches of my face and I did not dare answer him for fear of betraying myself with an obviously foreign accent. Grim saved that situation by a trick as old as Hebron is — a trick that has saved armies before now.

He started to sing, choosing the lilting air the Hebron men love most, and making up the words to it, as nearly every singer does in that town of surviving customs.

> Oh, fortunate and famous are the men of El-Kalil!
> Allah watches them! Oh, Allah watches them!
> They are gallant to the stranger, to the stranger in the gates!
> Allah watches them! Oh, Allah watches them!

They caught the refrain and throat after throat took it up, beginning to sway a little in time to it and ceasing from the cattle-thrust all in one direction that was pinning them choked and helpless between walls. The man who wanted my blood laughed and began to sing too.

> Hither came Er-Rahman [Abraham], hither across deserts,
>   hither to make friendship with the men of El-Kalil!
>   Allah watches them! Oh, Allah watches them!
>   None else had befriended him. None had housed the
> stranger. Wondering he wandered to the tents of El-Kalil!
>   Allah watches them! Oh, Allah watches them!

Now the whole street was thundering the refrain and a rival singer took up the story of Abraham, for rivalry is keen among the bards of that place and no "sweet singer" lets a new man hold attention long if he can help it. And because the men of El-Kalil, like those of other cities, have their own moods and their own expressions of emotion they began to form groups and face inward, little by little easing the forward pressure as the men in the rear made room to sway and swing in time to the improvised ballad.

Grim did not waste time then. He grabbed me by the arm and hauled me into a doorway, kicked on the door until a woman opened and then without a word of explanation rushed past her up a rickety old stair-way to the roof. We were followed by a dozen men before she could get the door closed again and whether Grim knew the way or not they showed it to us — up over roof after roof — flat ones, domed ones, — along copings — jumping here and there across dark ditches that were Hebron "streets" and frequently scaring women off the roofs in front of us — pursued all the way by the thunder of the song Grim started.

Allah watches them! Oh! Allah watches them!

You could have recognized the Ghetto by the change of smells. But there was a glow of light there too, and rival music snarling from somewhere out of sight, tinny and thin but carrying its theme through endless bars instead of pausing to repeat, as Arab music does.

WE LAY at the end of a roof and looked over — down on a sight so weird that the modern world and all that belonged to it became a dream forthwith. Not that this looked real; there was nothing real any longer. Life was a myth. We were dreamers, peering down into the vale of dreams.

Have you ever seen the ancient Jewish costume? Purple and apricot-color — ancient Jews in turbans, with their long, curled earlocks, and the gestures that signify race-consciousness refusing not to be expressed? And the Jewish boys, togged out like their sires, gawky and awkward in the ancient costume, full of all the fiery zeal of their race and not yet trained to self-suppression?

It was a courtyard below us, connected to the street by that dark passage we had entered the evening before. The passage was still as black as pitch, but open windows facing on the court bathed that in golden-yellow light. Framed in the windows there were Jewesses — Esthers, Rachels, Rebeccas — crowding for a front view, bejeweled with long gold ear-rings, open-mouthed, afraid — gleaming-eyed women.

There was a committee of Arabs, thirty or forty strong, armed to the teeth, standing back to the wall around two sides of the court, eying the whole scene with owlish attention to detail. Back to the entrance of the passageway stood Ali Baba, with his sixteen sons behind him in a semi-circle; and behind them again, dimly discernible in shadow was an old *muballir* chanting nasally from a copy of the Koran held with both hands on his lap. The Jewish music, out of the darkness in the corner opposite was, presumably by way of opposition to that heresy.

The most striking figure of them all was Cohen, standing in the midst, facing Ali Baba, with the Chief Rabbi on his right hand and another on his left. He wore a turban, to which false ringlets had been pinned, and was nearly naked to the waist, his skin gleaming in the mellow light.

They had togged him out like an Orthodox Jew, but there was a girdle about his waist and all the upper part of his clothing hung down from that, so that he looked like a butcher about to slay according to ancient ritual.

The armed Arabs began to grow impatient and two or three of them called out, but I could not catch what was said. The cry was taken up by the younger Jews behind, and without waiting for the *muballir* to finish chanting Ali Baba stepped up to Cohen and breathed fire on him.

Instantly the whole of Cohen's torso seemed to leap into flame — blue flame, of the sort that dances on a Christmas pudding — flame that crawled snake-fashion, changing shape to disappear in one place and appear in another. The Arabs roared delight; the women shrilled in the windows, and the young Jews at the rear set up a dogfight din that might have meant anything.

Cohen took something in his hands — a sponge it might have been — pressed it to his breast, and that, too, caught fire. The flame died down on his body and flickered out, but the thing in his hands burned on. Ali Baba bowed to the ground in front of it, all his sons following suit; then the sons made way down their midst for him and turned behind him four abreast as he started for the street. The band of Jewish musicians struck up a lively air with cymbals, and Cohen started after them, followed by two Rabbis and at least two hundred other Jews, all chanting, while the Arabs waited to come last, flashing their swords in air and yelling in praise of Allah.

The last I saw of the procession just then was a ball of fire in the black passage that rose and fell as Cohen tossed it and the weird sheen on his arms and breast as the blue light flashed on them.

"Let's go!" said Grim and we crossed by an arch above a dark street that was all one voice of roaring men, who milled and mobbed to get out of the way of the fire-gift, urged to it by men on wiry gray ponies who pricked at them with spear-tips and cursed in the name of the Most High. The Jewish music penetrated through and above the din like the wail of forgotten ages; but every minute or so every other sound was suddenly drowned beneath the Moslem roar that answers all arguments, confounds all doubters, satisfies all requirements.

"*Allahu akbar! La illahah il-allah!* God is great. There is no god but God!"

We got down into a side street by a wall and set of steps and ran in a circuit to head off the crowd. But it was useless to try to reach the mosque by the south entrance, for every available inch of footing along the route was crammed with men, who sang in groups, each group with a soloist making up songs for them and all thundering the refrains, so that the winding, dark street-canyons were one interminable roar. And there was a reek of human sweat you could have leaned against.

But there was an old minaret, disused because unsafe, that overlooked the whole of the Haram court, and whose good, stout olive-wood door, hinged like a treasure-chest, was only fastened by a cheap brass Brummagem padlock.

Grim broke that with the first rock handy and we climbed the stone stairs that rocked now and then in their setting, scaring out bats that like to haunt disused buildings. We emerged on a rickety platform, whose broken iron railing hung loose above a sea of heads.

The whole Haram court was chock-a-block with men. You could see de Crespigny's horse nodding and champing nervously outside in the street, where one of the policemen held him. The rest of the police were up beside de Crespigny on the mosque steps behind the Sheikh, whose gaunt, Old Testament face was a picture of mingled dignity and nervousness.

On the steps below the Sheikh, but leaving a narrow gangway for him, were about twenty notables; and there was a narrow cleared space, two men wide perhaps, leading all the way from them to the South Gate. There was plenty of light on the scene; for, besides the great iron bracket-lanterns, many of the men had kerosene lanterns, swung on sticks to keep them safe above the struggling crowd.

We were none too soon. The circuit we had made had used up time. We could hear the cymbals already, and the chanting penetrating through the roar from Moslem throats. In another minute I caught sight of a dancing ball of blue fire; and then, through a wide gap between two roofs, I saw Cohen.

He said afterwards that he was in deadly fear all the while, but I believe he was enjoying himself. At intervals between tossing the fire and catching it he would bathe his arms in it, and wave them, blazing blue, until the crowd gasped. And he looked as solemn as if he had been born to the trade of making miracles.

Ali Baba and his gang of sixteen thieves marched on ahead of him with all the righteous dignity of men who have given back what they might not keep — there is no higher sanctity than that in El-Kalil — and, swinging to the left at the sharp turn by the gate, marched through like old-time priests, forming two abreast, now, because of the narrow passage. They came up the enormous entrance steps and paraded, dignified and solemn, straight up to the Sheikh, where Ali Baba bowed very low and said something — I couldn't hear what, though the crowd inside the Haram was absolutely still by that time.

But Cohen did not dare go past the seventh entrance step from the bottom, where a hole in the wall is, that they say — in order to pacify the Jews — connects like a whispering tube with the tomb of Abraham a hundred yards away beneath. No Jew dare go past that seventh step on pain of death.

He stood on it and tossed the fire, while Ali Baba did the heralding and the music of the Jews outside blended with a roar of excited voices. Then Ali Baba started back to carry the fire to the mosque, since no Jew must come nearer and Grim caught hold of my arm.

"We'll miss the big scene if we stay here. Come!"

Down these rickety steps we went again among the bats and bugs, hurrying all the faster because of the risk of falling masonry — clambered by a lean-to up on to the same wide-topped wall that had stood us in good stead the night before — ran along it to the end, unchallenged for two reasons: we were up in shadow above the dancing lights, and the crowd was intoxicated with the sight of something else. The fire-gift was in Ali Baba's hands now, being carried up the narrow path between them all.

At the end of the wall we slid down a buttress and passed into the mosque through the Sheikh's own private door. But there we were nonplused for the moment. You could have walked on the heads of men who sat, all facing away from us in the direction of the south door, where the Sheikh was welcoming the fire-gift — a level, multi-colored lake of heads.

No one noticed us. We slipped along the wall as far as the pulpit. The little wooden door at the foot of it was hanging on the latch and we slipped through unseen, to stand in deep shadow on the upper steps with a view of every square foot of all that great mosque.

AT THE far end, not thirty feet from the southern door, is a little arched recess in the wall with an ornamental brass lamp hanging in it. Beneath the lamp is a perfectly round hole that leads through the solid black rock to the cave beneath. The hole is about twelve inches in diameter and the Moslems kneel and pray through it to Father Abraham, and drop little messages down to him written on slips of paper. There was a space kept clear around that hole and a gangway from it to the door.

Up that gangway presently, preceded by the Sheikh, came Ali Baba carrying the fire, shaking it to make the flame burn fiercely, and the roar that God is Great went up into the mosque roof from the throats of the seated throng by way of greeting. The Sheikh stopped at the hole and turned to face the congregation.

"Behold!" he cried out. "Before the eyes of all of you that which was taken is returned!" At that Ali Baba — rather lingering, as if he hated to be parted from his treasure — dropped the blue fire down the hole and for about a minute nothing happened, while the congregation watched in utter silence. Then however the ten or twenty thousand little slips of paper on the cave floor caught alight and a column of blue-gray smoke emerged like the jinnee out of the fisherman's jar in the Arabian Nights' tale — formed a great query mark in mid-air — and rose leisurely to mushroom and spread against the roof.

That was a true miracle if ever men sat and saw one. The congregation moaned like the wind in a forest, swaying their bodies and murmuring that God is great. Ali Baba went out by the south door, minded, I expect, to tell the crowd outside what marvels had been seen to happen. And the Sheikh, minded too, to make the most of things while the impression was still at its height, began to thread his way toward the pulpit.

"We'd better beat it quick!" said Grim and to save time we vaulted over the pulpit-rail into the utter darkness between the back wall and the door we entered by. There we stayed to hear the Sheikh do what he could to keep the crowd quiet until morning.

But the Sheikh had had a change of heart since Grim last talked with him. Something in his lean, mean face made me suspicious the minute he reached the pulpit and paused to look about him while the congregation faced his way. There was a thin smile and a sneer; and a strange light in his eye.

"My God! He's going back on us!" Grim whispered. But we stayed to listen. I suppose most men would rather hear themselves condemned to death than have the sentence pronounced in their absence.

You could see in a second how the Sheikh had argued it. The miracle had happened. The fire-gift was returned. His own reputation in the community was likely to be stronger now than ever. The only risk to him was that certain men in the secret might betray him, and of those Ali Baba and his sons would obviously keep the secret for their own sake. Why not then, get rid of the handful of white men who were almost sure to talk in clubs and messes? It was easy enough.

"Allah is all-majesty!" he began, and paused while they murmured a response. "Ye have seen. Your eyes have seen. Your ears heard the vision from my lips. Ye know now that these dogs of Jews of El-Kalil are to be spared awhile. But I have yet to see the vision — I have yet to hear the word explaining why the Moslems of Jerusalem should lay their necks beneath the feet of Jews, at the bidding of alien rulers. What says the Book? 'And God drove back the infidels in their wrath; they won no advantage; for God is strong, mighty!' No vision yet has told me why the aliens in this place — are they not few, and ye so many — should stand between you and your faith in an hour when —"

"Here! Let's beat it quick!" said Grim and led the way.

We shinnied up the wall again and down by the lower wall that Grim had used the night before. The same roar was throbbing in the main streets, louder than before if anything; but Grim knew all the byways, and we made for the Governorate with the fear of death dogging our heels, every swell of the tumult sounding in our ears like the beginning of the end and every deep shadow looking like an ambush.

I don't think Grim had anything in mind except to get back to the Governorate. I know I hadn't. The place where a man's friends are, or ought to be, draws him when the hunt begins as his home earth draws the fox. The fact that the Governorate couldn't possibly be defended for ten minutes made no difference; that was home and we ran for it sobbing for breath, I with a stitch in my side like a knife-wound, and Grim lending a hand at intervals to pull me when wind gave out altogether.

And in the end we reached the widening street, where the city leaves off and suburb begins, at almost exactly the same moment as de Crespigny, riding well-content with his eight good, dark-skinned legionaries tramping along behind him.

"What's your hurry?" he asked.

Grim laid a hand on his saddle, fighting for breath to speak with.

"The Sheikh's gone back on us!" he gasped. "He feels he's safe — wants to keep the secret in the family — the swine's advising them to scupper us!"

"All up, eh?" said de Crespigny. "Well, we gave 'em a run for their money! Take a stirrup each and run beside me." He turned to the faithful eight and gave his orders in an unchanged voice:

" 'Tention! Quick march! Double!"

CHAPTER XII

"Let's have supper now and drink to them seventeen thieves!"

WE STOPPED at the jail and brought the guard away, jailers and all, leaving the prisoners to whatever fate awaited them. Most mobs empty the jail first thing, if only for the sake of mischief, but de Crespigny took care that the outer door was locked and bolted.

Cohen arrived in a state of jubilant joy two or three minutes after we reached the Governorate; and then we had a surprise. Ali Baba turned up with his sixteen sons.

"What do you want here?" asked de Crespigny.

"They are coming to kill you officers."

"Well?"

"I and my sons have pledged ourselves to be your friends. Give us guns. We will fight for you until the end comes."

"I've got no guns, O father of true promises."

"Taib. We have knives."

There wasn't any comment you could make exactly. De Crespigny shook hands with him and Jones posted them in the hall, where in a free-for-all fight against an invading mob knives could be used to the best advantage.

Cohen disappeared, and came back ten minutes later with the bitterly protesting Scots nurse. He could not have brought her by force, for she was stronger than any two of him, but he had threatened to murder the doctor unless he ordered her away to the Governorate; and the doctor had smiled and given in, saying that the presence of a woman might help the boys. But she was angry. My word, she was angry! And she set about fixing up a first-aid place at once in de Crespigny's bedroom, although I did not see what good that would do if the mob came on in earnest.

And sure enough, they came within the hour, bringing torches with them, roaring up the street like bulls turned loose. They paused before the jail to hold a consultation, but after five minutes of noise decided not to open it; then came on again, singing about the swords of El-Kalil. And because it was dark and you couldn't guess their numbers, it seemed as if the whole East were surging along to swamp and roll over us and surge along forever.

"I'll take mine on the steps with the police," said Jones and went out through the front door, where we heard the breech-bolts clicking as he examined the men's rifles in the window-light.

"Poor old Jonesy's got the wind up badly!" said de Crespigny. "I'll go out to the gate and talk to them. Grim, will you do what you can to hold the place if they scough me?"

He followed Jones out through the door and Grim sent me to the roof with a revolver and orders to use my wits if I had any left. So I saw what took place better than any one did.

De Crespigny mounted the wall and stood this time, for they could not have seen him otherwise, while the mob milled and sang songs at him. You could see their eyes by the light of the lanterns they carried — that and the sheen on swords and knives, nothing more. It was a long time before he could make his voice heard and then they laughed at him, which is a very bad sign among Moslems.

"What do you want?" he demanded.

"Rifles!"

"I have none."

"Liar! Father of lies! Kill the liar and loot his stores!"

De Crespigny held one hand up for silence and because they were used to giving him a hearing they gave him a last one now.

"Now for your own sakes, don't be fools! You can kill me; that's easy. You can loot the Governorate, although you'll find that tough work and not worth while. Then you can start for Jerusalem; and the Sikhs will meet you on the way! I've done my best for you. If you'll go back to your homes now there shall be no reprisals for this night's work. Go home, and act like sensible men!"

Some one threw a rock at him, but missed and it broke a lower window. They laughed and he held up a hand for silence again. It was then that I heard a row like the grumble of far-off thunder and looking to the right saw a string of swiftly moving lights — very strong lights, one behind the other, heading this way from Jerusalem. That was Sikhs in lorries; it couldn't be anything else. They were coming like a fourth-alarm turn-out to a fire.

A minute later, while de Crespigny was trying to make himself heard above the growing tumult, the men on the crowd's edge heard too, and looked and yelled. Ten minutes later ten great lorries came to a halt in line in an utterly empty street in front of the Governorate, disgorging two machine guns and more hairy Sikhs than you would have believed could be possibly crowded into that space.

The Sikhs were angry. They had been skirmishing for a day and a night without sleep. They wanted nothing on earth so much as a crowd to glut their temper on and stood about outside, grumbling their disappointment. But one enormous man with a beard like the man's on the chutney-bottle in the grocer's window thrust his way into the Governorate, calling aloud for Jimgrim.

"Ah!" he exclaimed at sight of him and came to attention. "Not dead, then, *sahib!* And the man I was to reckon with — that Ali Baba person — where is he?"

Grim introduced them and the eyes of Sikh and Arab met for thirty full seconds.

Then Narayan Singh the Sikh grinned hugely and thrust his bayonet forward. Ali Baba answered the threat by touching his knife and pointed to his sixteen sons.

"The more the better!" said Narayan Singh, perfectly ready to accept odds of seventeen to one.

"Inshallah!"

"We will see, whenever the time comes!"

"Inshallah!" repeated Ali Baba sweetly.

"Lovin' couple, ain't they!" put in Cohen. "Say; don't you fellows ever eat supper in this joint? I'm dyin' o' thirst! What time is it?"

"Ah!" Grim laughed. "That reminds me; here's your watch back. I allow you've won the bet. Where's mine?"

"Gimme mine first."

Grim obeyed and Cohen pocketed the thing.

"Like to kid yourself, don't you! Think I'll part with yours? Nothin' doing! I'll keep this blame thing for a souvenir — souvenir o' the first time I was made a stark starin' sucker out of and wasn't sorry! But say; let's have supper now and drink to them seventeen thieves!"

THE END

www.ingramcontent.com/pod-product-compliance
Lightning Source LLC
Chambersburg PA
CBHW020700180626
46816CB00003B/1374